FAKE OUT!

"Pick 'em up!" captain LaMont Jackson yelled at his teammates, the Jefferson Patriots. "Press 'em

Other books in the **HOOPS** series:

HALF-COURT
HERO

Kirk Marshall

BALLANTINE BOOKS • NEW YORK

Special thanks to Steve Clark.

RLI: <u>VL: 6 & up</u>
IL: 6 & up

For Jacqueline Uva Dinas,
a tiny dribbler.

ONE

"We are number one! We are number one!"

Brian Davis, Jefferson High's six-foot-eight-inch star center, listened to the chant filtering through the walls of the Patriots' gym. The place was packed.

It was almost game time, and Brian and his teammates were standing behind a glass door leading to the court. The catchy chant grew louder.

"Man, our fans are right," Reggie Dupree said, peeking through the door.

"Yeah, we're twelve and two," said stocky junior guard Tony Zarella, adjusting his white game jersey. "The way we've been kicking butts lately, we ain't gonna lose another game."

"That's cool, bro," Dupree said, smiling. The slender black guard bashed forearms with Tony.

1

The forearm bash had replaced high-fives on the Patriots. "We are *bad!*"

The other players laughed, and Brian smiled.

"Hey, we're ranked number five in the whole state of Indiana," Tony added, buttoning his blue warm-up jacket, "but I can't think of four teams better than us."

"There ain't none," Reggie said.

"All right!" said Cisco Vega, a six-two junior sub. He bashed forearms with Tony and Reggie.

"Yeah, guys, but we're only as good as our last game," said the team's captain, LaMont Jackson, from near the door. The six-two black forward was preparing to lead the team onto the court. "Too many dudes think they can whip everybody, then end up losing to some wimps."

"Not us, man," Cisco said. "We got it together."

"That's cool," said Clarence Reed, a six-three black forward, "but we gotta kick butts every game. And we gotta keep passing the ball to Davis. Dude can shoot."

Reed pulled the protective goggles he wore down over his eyes and bashed forearms with Cisco Vega.

"Davis is a star," Tony said, smiling and using the glass door to fix his bushy hair.

"Yeah, but he's ugly," said Jeff Burgess, a reserve center and a lineman during football season.

"Don't need good looks to shoot thirty-foot jumpers," said redheaded Terry Hanson. The senior playmaker smiled. "Davis proves that."

The other players laughed and shoved Brian.

"Yeah, but Davis is averaging almost thirty points a game," Tony said.

"He's a gen-u-ine living legend," Reggie added, playfully elbowing Brian.

"Gimme a break, guys," Brian said, buttoning his warm-up jacket and smiling at Reggie and Tony.

Tony and Reggie had been Brian's best friends since last summer when he moved with his mom to Indianapolis from the small country town of Paintville, Indiana. They had also helped him adjust to Jefferson High, a big city school.

The team's laughter faded as their two coaches joined them from the downstairs locker room.

"It's nice to hear so much confidence," said head coach Tom Ford. The youthful coach was a former star at Jefferson and an All-American guard at Purdue. "But when you're one of the top ten teams in the state, everybody plays harder against you."

"We can handle it, coach," Tony said.

"Man, we're a regular powerhouse," added black sophomore guard Alvin Woolridge.

"Yeah, just ask Westside," Terry Hanson said. "Those dudes were undefeated before we trashed 'em."

The players shouted and exchanged forearm bashes.

"Guys, it was a close overtime game," LaMont said in his usual calm voice. The team settled down. "We gotta be ready for anything."

"Especially tonight," added heavyset black assistant coach Mel Williams. The six-five former college star stroked his black and silver goatee and continued in his deep voice. "South Central's got some quick players, the type of dudes who been givin' us trouble all season."

"Let's quickly go over Central's scouting report," Coach Ford said, looking at the clipboard in his hands. "Dupree, what about Stan Corbett, the guy you'll be guarding?"

"Dude's a six-three white guard who's quick and likes to shoot three-pointers."

"The Central fans call him 'Stan the Man,'" Cisco said with a chuckle.

Some of the other players booed playfully.

Coach Ford continued. "Make him drive to the hoop where our big guys can swat away his shots."

"Yeah, our swat team," Terry said with a smile. "Reed, Jackson, and Davis can block anybody's shots."

The players cheered and exchanged forearm bashes.

"What about your man, Davis?" Coach Ford asked.

"Name's Walker Pyle," Brian said. He tried to remember what they had discussed about South Central at yesterday's practice. "He's a six-six black center who can really run fast. Scores a lot on lay-ups after their full-court press steals the ball."

"And speaking about their press," Coach Williams said in his baritone voice, "they've got a good one. Billy Sutherland is only five eight, but the dude's one of the quickest guards we're gonna see this season. Watch out for him."

"Boy's gotta catch me first," Reggie said, "and nobody's done that yet."

The preliminary game between the Jefferson and South Central B-teams ended in the gym and the teams were leaving the court. Brian listened as loud music from the Patriots' pep band drifted through the glass door. The varsity players huddled around the coaches.

"We're number five in the state," Coach Ford said. He stuck out his hand. "Let's try for number one."

Brian and his teammates slapped their hands on top of their coach's.

"Let's kick butt tonight!" shouted Terry Hanson.

"Man, these dudes are pushovers," Reggie added.

The team yelled "One, two, three, beat Central!" As they headed out, Brian wondered if they were serious enough. The last time they were overconfident they got clobbered by Gary Tech earlier in the season.

The Patriots ran onto the court and two thousand Jefferson rooters, many of them dressed in the school's colors of red, white, and blue, cheered wildly. The cheerleaders ran beside the players and waved pom-poms. The pep band played a loud fight song.

"Nothing beats playing at home," Tony said as they formed two lines for lay-ups.

Brian nodded, then waved at his mom and aunt, who always sat near the Patriots' bench.

The South Central Scarlet Knights, dressed in red warm-ups, raced onto the other end of the court. Several hundred of their rooters stood in the bleachers and cheered.

"Those dudes don't look so tough," Reggie said to Brian as they waited their turn in the lay-up line.

"Man, Sutherland's smaller than me," Wollridge said, pointing at the South Central playmaker.

"And that's small," Cisco said, running in for a shot.

The other Patriots laughed, and Brian hoped the Scarlet Knights were as lousy as his teammates figured.

After fifteen minutes of swishing long jumpers, Brian heard the buzzer and knew the game was about to start. He trotted to the bench with his teammates. The officials checked with the scorer, the cheerleaders yelled, and the players on both teams listened to final instructions from their coaches.

"South Central's real quick," Coach Ford reminded the Patriots, "so be ready for their full-court press."

"And make good passes," Coach Williams added.

Brian and the Patriots' usual starting lineup of LaMont and Clarence Reed at forward and Reggie and Terry Hanson at guard walked to the midcourt jump-ball circle. The Jefferson rooters rose and began chanting for their team.

Reggie leaned close to Brian so he could be

heard over the noise. "After tonight, we could be number one," he said, smiling.

"We gotta win first," Brian shouted.

"No sweat," Reggie said, bashing forearms with Davis, who had a confident smile on his face.

"Yeah, these guys are nothing," Terry said.

But, as the starting five for the South Central Scarlet Knights walked over to the jump-ball circle, Brian saw the determined looks on their faces and knew the game was going to be tough.

Walker Pyle, the Knights' tall center, nodded at Brian and shook his hand. Brian noticed his Patriot teammates were ignoring the other Central starters.

The official tossed up the ball between the two centers. Brian stretched as high as he could, but Pyle out-jumped him by several inches. He tapped the ball to six-three guard Stan 'the Man' Corbett, who began dribbling.

"Pick up your men," LaMont shouted to the Patriots.

Davis stayed with Pyle and ran downcourt to play defense. His teammates found their men and did the same.

South Central tried to set up its offense, but the Scarlet Knights were nervous. Corbett fumbled the ball and stopped dribbling. Reggie hounded him and forced the big Central guard to pass wildly crosscourt. LaMont intercepted the ball.

"Fast break!" shouted Coach Ford from the bench.

LaMont tossed a perfect outlet pass to Reggie at midcourt. Brian and Reed raced downcourt in

the outside wing positions. Reggie tricky dribbled
past Corbett, stopped at the far free-throw line,
and snapped a bounce pass to Brian cutting to the
hoop. Brian took two giant steps and slam-dunked
the ball, giving Jefferson the lead 2–0.

The Jefferson fans cheered. Brian ran back
downcourt and bashed forearms with his teammates.

"I told you these dudes are nothing," Reggie
said.

"Hey!" LaMont suddenly shouted. He pointed at
Walker Pyle, who was streaking toward Central's
basket.

Corbett lofted a length-of-the-court pass to
Pyle.

Brian pumped his legs as fast as they could go.
He caught up with the speedy Pyle, reached up,
and blocked the lay-up shot. The ball bounced
over to Terry, who began dribbling back toward
the Patriots' basket.

"Way to go, Davis!" Cisco shouted from the
bench.

"In your face," Reggie said to Pyle as they both
ran downcourt.

Terry called out a play and the Patriots set up
their offense against Central's man-to-man defense. Brian made some offensive fakes and feints
along the baseline. He saw Pyle fall off balance
and cut past him toward the free-throw line. Terry
faked a pass to LaMont and zipped the ball to
Brian, who swished a fifteen foot jumper.

The score was Jefferson 4 and South Central 0.
A deafening cheer filled the gym.

"This is easy," Terry shouted to Brian as they ran back downcourt.

Brian guarded Pyle closely and watched as the Patriots stayed with their men. Then he noticed Reggie playing away from Corbett, who was standing beyond the three-point line.

"Come on, 'Stan the Man', " Reggie taunted, his arms at his sides, "shoot the ball."

Corbett didn't hesitate. He swished a twenty-footer.

The score was now Jefferson 4 and Central 3, and the Knights' rooters cheered.

"Don't do that again," LaMont said to Reggie as they changed from defense to offense.

"The dude was lucky," Reggie said.

"Maybe, but play him tight."

"No problem," Reed said, grabbing the ball and preparing to inbound it.

While Brian and LaMont jogged downcourt to play offense, South Central set up a man-to-man press all over the court.

"Help!" Reed shouted from out-of-bounds. He suddenly couldn't find anybody to pass the ball to. "Press! Press!"

Both officials blew their whistles and signaled five seconds had gone by. The Patriots lost the ball by not getting it inbounds on time. The Central rooters cheered.

"Man, get open for a pass," Reed shouted at his teammates. "They're pressing us!"

"Our fault, Reed," LaMont said. "Run the press play next time, guys."

While Brian and the other Patriots were discussing the press play, Central inbounded the ball to Corbett. Stan the Man faked Reggie out of his socks, dribbled beyond the three-point circle, and swished another long jump shot.

The Scarlet Knights took the lead 6–4.

"Watch out for the press!" Coach Ford shouted from the bench. "Work the play!"

Brian and the Patriots raced to their positions on the court. Reed grabbed the ball and looked at his teammates, but again the quick South Central defenders were guarding closely.

"Help out Reed!" LaMont shouted from his position downcourt. "Go to the ball!"

Brian, standing at midcourt, ran toward Clarence. But Reed panicked and tossed a wild pass that Walker Pyle intercepted ten feet from the hoop. The Central center slam-dunked the ball, and the score was now South Central 8 and Jefferson 4.

Coach Ford slammed a towel onto the floor.

Reed grabbed the ball before Central could set up its press and passed it to Reggie on the court.

"Run the play," LaMont shouted as he ran downcourt.

Brian ran to midcourt and raised his hands for a pass. But as he turned toward Reggie, he saw Billy Sutherland, Central's five-foot-eight-inch guard, form a double team with Stan Corbett. Reggie was trapped.

"Dupree!" Brian shouted. But it was too late.

Sutherland lashed out with his right hand and slapped the ball away from Reggie. Corbett grabbed the ball and passed it to Walker Pyle, who was racing toward the basket. Brian watched helplessly as Pyle slam-dunked the ball for the second play in a row.

The score was now South Central 10 and Jefferson 4.

The Scarlet Knights clapped and high-fived one another. Coach Ford called timeout.

"Man, this stinks," Reggie said as he slumped next to Brian on the bench.

"Come on, guys, wake up," LaMont said, toweling off. "We gotta think out there."

Coach Ford reviewed the team's special play for pressing defenses. As he listened, Brian noticed the Jefferson fans were stunned into silence by the score.

The time-out ended and the Patriots trudged onto the court. South Central ran back onto the floor.

"Work the play," LaMont said. "Take care of the ball."

The official handed the ball to Reed, who slapped it as a signal for the Patriots to begin their press play.

"Everybody cut!" Coach Ford shouted.

As they had practiced many times, Brian and his teammates ran the press offense. Reggie and Terry set picks for each other near where Reed was standing. Then Hanson cut toward Reed and received a pass.

Brian saw Corbett and Sutherland about to double-team Hanson. He stood at midcourt and waved his arms. Terry saw him and fired a baseball pass to Brian.

Brian caught the ball and turned toward La-
Mont downcourt. But almost immediately he
found himself being double-teamed by Corbett
and Sutherland. Central's speedy player seemed to
be everywhere.

Faking a long pass to LaMont, Brian tried to
dribble between the two defenders. But his legs
became tangled and he lost his balance. At the
same time, Sutherland slapped the ball away and
began dribbling toward his basket.

Pyle raced downcourt, caught a pass from
Sutherland, and laid the ball into the basket. Reed,
hanging back after inbounding the ball to Hanson,
fouled Pyle on the shot.

The South Central players high-fived one another.

The score was now Central 12 and Jefferson 4.

"My fault," Brian said to his teammates as they
lined up for Pyle's free throw. He turned and
watched as Corbett stepped over to Reggie.

"Ain't so easy now, is it boy?" Corbett said.

Reggie started toward Stan the Man, but La-
Mont held him back. Corbett walked away, smiling.

"Save it for the game, man," LaMont said.

"This is embarrassing," Terry said.

After Pyle swished his free throw, Reed slapped
the ball and his teammates cut to their positions in
the press offense. Dupree received a pass from
Reed and tricky dribbled past Corbett and Sutherland toward Jefferson's hoop. The Patriots' rooters cheered as their team finally made it across
the midcourt line again.

South Central pressed just as tightly in the

halfcourt area. Reggie and Terry dribbled for nearly a minute as Brian, LaMont, and Reed faked and feinted but couldn't get free. Finally, unable to pass, Terry launched a twenty-foot jump shot.

The ball hit the backboard and swished through the hoop for a three-point basket. The score was now South Central 13 and Jefferson 7.

For the rest of the first quarter, Brian and his teammates struggled against the Scarlet Knights' full-court press. Sutherland stole the ball four more times, twice from Brian as he tried to dribble across midcourt, and the other Central players stuck to the Jefferson starters like glue. The Patriots scored only when Corbett fouled LaMont and he swished both free throws.

After one quarter, the score was South Central 23 and Jefferson 9.

"We can do it, guys," Cisco Vega said hopefully as Brian and the other stunned starters slumped on the bench.

"That Corbett dude's asking for it," Reggie said, toweling off.

"He's just playing hard," Coach Ford said above the pep band's music. He looked up at the scoreboard. "We've dug ourselves a hole and we'll have to climb out of it."

The Patriots tried by outscoring Central by four points over the last three quarters, but the Knights' full-court press still caused lots of problems—especially for Brian, who had trouble passing and dribbling. He fumbled away passes, passed wildly, and dribbled off his feet. When Jefferson *did* manage to get the ball over the midcourt line, Davis scored on several long jump shots.

Brian's teammates also played poorly against the full-court pressure defense. LaMont, Clarence, and the other tall players had trouble handling the ball smoothly. The subs also fumbled the ball often.

The Knights, however, scored on easy lay-ups.

The final score was South Central 80 and Jefferson 70. Although Brian scored thirty-three points and grabbed sixteen rebounds, the Patriots' winning streak ended at seven. Their ranking in the state high school ratings was sure to drop.

After the game, Brian and the other Patriots shook hands reluctantly with the smiling Central players, then trudged to the locker room. The Jefferson fans left the gym quietly.

Coach Ford was surprisingly calm after the game.

"They outplayed us," said the coach in the gloomy locker room, "But now we know what to work on in practice."

"Looks like you dudes and me are gonna be doing some ball-handling drills," Coach Williams said. The heavyset assistant forced a smile and followed Coach Ford out of the locker room.

"We can hardly wait," Tony said as Brian and the Patriots peeled off their sweaty uniforms in silence.

TWO

"What happened against South Central?" "How could you guys lose to those wimps?" "Don't you feel embarrassed?"

Brian and his teammates arrived at school on Monday and immediately faced a chorus of these questions from the kids and teachers. The weekend hadn't lessened the pain of losing.

"It's like we have a losing record," Reggie said as he walked in the hallway with Brian and Tony.

"Remember what LaMont said, we're only as good as our last game," Tony said.

"In that case, we stink," Reggie said.

"We played like B-team players," Brian said. For the first time since basketball season began, he tried to avoid the other kids at school. But at six eight, it was hard.

15

"Corbett burned me for thirty-three points," Reggie said. "And, the dude's not *that* good."

"Corbett made five three-pointers," Brian said, "but it was Central's press that made us look like rookies."

"Sutherland's a damn quick guard, too," Tony said, stroking the stubble on his face.

"Picked me clean five times," said Brian, shaking his head. "I never saw the little dude until he was dribbling away with the ball."

Mr. Rhodes, the plump little gray-haired principal, walked around a corner and shook his head at them.

"Boys, I'm on my way to a citywide school-board meeting," the principal said. His round face was creased into a frown. "I'm afraid I'll be asked the same question by the other principals. Nobody likes a loser."

The principal left and Brian stared after him. "We better win tomorrow night to keep Mr. Rhodes from getting depressed."

"Zellinger High's team ain't nothing," Tony said as they neared their classroom. "What do you expect from any school that calls its team the Zebras?"

"Betcha those dudes press us all over the court," Reggie said.

Brian nodded. "Wouldn't you? We made thirty-two errors Friday night and looked like wimps doing it."

They walked into English class and immediately Miss Pinchot, the gray-haired and narrow-faced teacher, pointed at a stack of paperback books on her desk.

"Boys, get yourselves copies of Steinbeck's *Grapes of Wrath*," she said in a nasal voice. "There's no full-court press here so you shouldn't drop them." She chuckled.

"That's cute, Miss Pinchot," Tony said, handing copies of the book to Brian and Reggie. "Real cute."

"We all learn from our mistakes," Miss Pinchot said, "in English class as well as on the basketball court. And you boys obviously have lots to learn after the way South Central played."

"We know," Tony said as he walked to his seat.

In the locker room that afternoon, Brian and his teammates changed slowly into their practice gear. The Patriots were taking the loss hard.

"Man, you'd think we hadn't won a game all season," Alvin Woolridge complained as he laced his high-tops. "Only thing folks are talkin' about is the South Central loss."

"Best way to shut them dudes up," Reed said, adjusting his goggles, "is to kick butts next game."

"I'm with Reed," Brian said, slamming his locker shut. "We gotta play hard and beat Zellinger tomorrow."

"And we gotta work hard on these ball-handling drills today," LaMont said. "Only kindergarten teams make thirty-two errors in a game."

While Brian and his teammates shot baskets before practice began, Coach Ford called Dupree and Hanson over to his office at one end of the gym. Two minutes later, they returned to the court, shocked expressions on their faces.

"Man, I'm flunking algebra," Reggie said. "Coach talked with Mr. Rhodes about everybody's grades."

"I got an F in U. S. History," Terry said, shaking his head. "Coach says we better pass our final exams next week or we can kiss basketball good-bye for the rest of the season."

"Can you get ready for the exams in one week?" Brian asked.

"Man, you kiddin'?" Reggie said. "Algebra and me don't get along."

"I'm a month behind with my history reading," Terry said. "No way I can catch up in a week."

A few minutes later, Coach Ford gathered the team at midcourt. "I don't have to ask what kind of day you had," the coach said.

"We've been taking heat about the South Central game, too," Coach Williams said.

"Forget about the loss and concentrate on correcting our ball-handling mistakes," Coach Ford said. "That means passing and catching as well as dribbling. We did such a lousy job with all of 'em, it looked like we never faced a press before."

"But don't worry," Coach Williams added. "Ball handling can be learned."

Coach Ford cleared his throat. "Now, about grades and final exams," he said. "Some of you are in trouble."

"Man, today's our day for bad news," Alvin Woolridge said, shifting his weight nervously.

"You're okay, Woolridge," Coach Williams said, "and so are most of you." The heavyset assistant stared at Reggie and Terry. "But some dudes haven't been hitting the books."

"Hanson and Dupree are the only ones close to becoming ineligible for basketball," Coach Ford said. "And we're going to do something about it before it's too late."

"Here comes the real bad news," Reggie said.

"We've always been a team off the court as well as on it," Coach Ford continued, "so you guys are going to help one another with schoolwork. Brad Cunningham's a straight-A student in algebra. I'd like him to help Dupree get ready for his final exam."

The team looked at Brad, who adjusted his thick-lensed glasses and nodded. "Sure, Coach," he said. "We'll study at my house every day after practice. My mom won't mind."

"Thanks, man," Reggie said, bashing forearms with Brad.

"Davis, you're doing okay in history," Coach Ford said, "so how about helping Hanson?"

"Sure, Coach, no sweat," Brian said.

"Way to go, guys," Coach Williams added. "With all-star tutors like these dudes, Dupree and Hanson oughtta make the honor roll."

The players booed and hissed playfully.

"Now, before Coach Williams works your butts off," Coach Ford said finally, "don't forget about tonight's game at Butler University. We've got tickets for all of you. It's like a field trip to check out the court where we'll play our sectional tournament games."

"Meet Coach Ford and me at seven o'clock in front of Gate E," Coach Williams added. "My main man in the Butler ticket office set us up with front row seats."

"Ohio State and Butler," Reggie said. "Man, I'm looking forward to the game."

"Dupree, you better raise your grades or all you'll be doing the rest of the season is watching games," Coach Ford said, smiling.

The players laughed and playfully shoved Reggie.

"Okay, gimme twenty laps around the court and then some flexibility exercises," Coach Williams said, smiling. "Then you're mine for some drills."

The players groaned, then trotted around the court.

"Man, even the drills seem tougher when we lose," Alvin said. "I ain't lookin' forward to this."

"Coach Williams has that look in his eyes," Tony said.

"Yeah," Cisco added as they ran, "like the Marine drill sergeant in *Full Metal Jacket.*"

Halfway through their laps, LaMont caught up with Brian and ran beside him.

"We always have a January slump," LaMont said, huffing and puffing. "The guys get tired and lose a few games. I ain't worried, though."

"I am," Brian said, sweat dripping off his face. "I hate to lose."

"Me, too, but sometimes it helps us get ready for the state tournament. We see our mistakes."

"I don't want to see 'em," Brian said. "Coach Williams gets all worked up and runs us to death with his drills."

"Ball handling ain't gonna kill you, homeboy," LaMont said. "Might even make you the tallest playmaker in Indiana." LaMont laughed and nudged Brian playfully.

While the players stretched their muscles, Coach Williams placed a dozen folding metal chairs down the middle of the court. Then he gathered the Patriots under one of the main baskets and handed each of them a ball.

"The idea is to dribble downcourt and between the chairs," said the black assistant coach. "Then dribble back doing the same thing."

"Keep your head up and try not to look at the ball," Coach Ford added. "Pretend you're being pressed."

"Piece of cake," Cisco said.

"Start by dribbling high like you would in the open," Coach Williams said. "Then, when I blow my whistle, change to a low dribble and make believe you're being closely guarded. Switch again on every whistle."

Following LaMont in a long line, Brian and the Patriots dribbled downcourt and around the chairs. The uneven patter of bouncing basketballs echoed in the old gym, as did Coach Williams's whistle blasts.

Nick Vanos, a six-four senior reserve center, was the first to bounce his ball off his foot. Husky

Jeff Burgess was next to muff the drill and run after his ball. Brian tried to control his ball by peeking at it while dribbling, but he bumped into one of the chairs, upending it. His ball rolled toward the bleachers.

"You big dudes are gonna dribble sometimes during games," Coach Williams shouted, "so work on these drills!"

"Come on, Davis," Coach Ford yelled, "you're the one the other teams will let dribble once they see you can't handle the ball."

Twenty minutes later Coach Williams changed drills.

"This one's called the 'zigzag drill,'" said the big coach as he cleared away the chairs. "Dribble downcourt in a zigzag pattern, first at an angle to the left for about ten feet, and then, after a crossover dribble, go at an angle to the right for about ten feet. When you reach the other end of the court, turn around and do it again."

The squad dribbled downcourt again, but this time in four different lines. The small players handled the ball well, but Brian and the other big guys had trouble.

"I'd be better off bouncing a football," Jeff Burgess said as he lost control of his ball again.

"Come on," LaMont shouted, "don't be klutzes."

"Big guys should hunch over when they dribble," Coach Ford yelled above the sound of the bouncing balls. "Makes it tougher for the defense to steal the ball."

Brian tried hard, but dribbling a ball was as awkward as trying to write left-handed.

"Hang in there, bro," Reed said. "I ain't no ball-handling wizard, neither."

"At least you're not kicking the ball all over the gym," Davis said, bouncing the ball off his foot again.

Brian and his teammates then practiced chest passes, bounce passes, and overhead passes until their arms ached. They also practiced the proper method of catching a ball.

"Keep your fingers spread and watch the ball all the way into your hands," Coach Williams said.

Finally, Coach Ford blew his whistle and dismissed the squad.

"Remember, seven o'clock at the Butler field-house," Coach Ford said, as the players trudged off the court. "I'll even buy burgers and fries after the game."

The Patriots perked up.

"Now you're talking, coach!" Tony said.

"Zarella nevers misses a free meal," said Cisco.

Brian and the others laughed, then ran downstairs to the locker room.

THREE

"Man, my feet are killin' me," Reggie said. "Coach Mel's drills are something else."

It was after practice and Brian, Reggie, and Tony were walking home. Night was about to fall and the air was cold.

"Lotsa drills and sore feet are what we deserve for losing," Tony said.

"Makes me wish we were undefeated," Reggie said.

"Then you'd have nothing to complain about, Dupree," Brian said, smiling.

"That's cool, man," Reggie said, limping along the sidewalk. "At least I wouldn't be hurting."

Brian and Tony laughed at their teammate.

"Yeah, but sweating through these drills is better then being cut because of bad grades," Tony said.

"You got that right," Reggie said, shaking his head.

"How'd you mess up algebra so bad?" asked Brian.

"Man, I don't understand that stuff. It's like a foreign language."

"Better get your act together or you can forget about hoops for a while," Tony said.

"Hang in there, Dupree, you'll make it with Cunningham on your side," Brian said. "Brad's a whiz with algebra."

"If you do flunk," Tony added with a smile, "maybe Coach Ford'll let you add up my points. That'll give you practice working with big numbers."

"Thanks for the job offer, guys," Reggie said, a disgusted look on his face, "but I'm gonna pass that exam."

"It's Hanson I'm really worried about," Brian said.

"Yeah, how's he gonna read four history books in one week?" Tony said.

The three Patriot teammates walked toward the local playground, which was lighted and crowded with kids even on a cold winter evening. Brian saw several groups of kids playing hoops on two nearby courts.

"Dudes gotta be crazy playing in this weather," Reggie said, blowing on his hands to warm them. "It's too cold to shoot a ball."

"Us shooters can put 'em up in any kind of weather," Brian said, looking down at Reggie.

"Ain't that the truth," Reggie said.

"Hey, look at the little kids," Tony said, pointing.

Brian turned toward the nearest asphalt court and saw two nine or ten-year-old kids shooting hoops with some bigger guys. They were playing a half-court game of four-on-four.

"Man, those little dudes can really dribble," Reggie said, stopping near the sagging chain-link fence surrounding the courts.

Brian watched as the two kids tricky dribbled around the bigger boys, then made fancy behind-the-back or between-the-legs passes to their teammates for easy baskets.

"They're dribbling circles around those big dudes," Reggie said, laughing.

"Yeah, and look who they're up against," Tony said.

"Roland Sims, Teddy Grissom, and some other dudes who used to play at Jefferson," Reggie said.

"Good players?" Brian asked.

"Used to be, but these little guys are out-playing 'em," Tony said, laughing. The bushy-haired junior yelled at the players on the court. "Hey Sims, you guys look sick."

Roland Sims, a lanky black kid in his early twenties, turned and shrugged his shoulders. "Man, these little kids are something else. Betcha even Davis can't stay with 'em."

"You hear that?" Reggie said, looking up at Brian. "The dude's challenging you, man."

"To play against some little kids?" Brian said, smiling. But then, he noticed the action on the court had stopped and everybody was staring at him.

"Do it, Davis," Tony said. "Show 'em your stuff."

"Coach Mel would be proud of you," Reggie said, laughing and playfully nudging Tony.

Brian smiled and shook his head, then walked through a hole in the fence and headed toward the court.

"Try and stay with these dudes," Roland said, gesturing at the two boys. "I seen you play, Davis, but ain't no way you gonna stop 'em."

Brian handed his schoolbooks to Tony, stretched his leg muscles, and turned to face the short dribblers. One of them was stocky and wore a hooded Indiana Pacers sweat shirt. The other was taller and skinnier with a freckled face.

"Take my place," Sims told Brian. "It's four against four."

Brian nodded, then crouched into a defensive stance and got ready to guard the freckle-faced kid. Brian couldn't help laughing. He straightened and looked at Roland.

"He's just a kid," Davis said, gesturing at the boy.

"Yeah, but the dude can play," Sims said.

Brian shook his head and figured he might as well go along with the joke. He got back into his defensive position and nodded at the freckle-faced kid.

From the moment the kid started dribbling, Brian knew he was in trouble. The ten-year-old controlled the ball equally well with either hand and dribbled better than any guard the Patriots had played against so far.

"Go get him, Davis," Tony shouted between fits of laughter.

Brian crouched as low as he could, slid his feet across the court, and tried to stay with the ten-year-old hotshot. But the kid dribbled the ball between his legs and around his back so fast Brian nearly fell on his butt.

"Coach Mel oughta see this," Reggie said, shoving Tony and laughing until he was almost crying.

When Brian tried to steal the ball and grabbed nothing but air, the freckle-faced ball handler whipped a between-the-legs pass to his stocky friend. The other boy then passed the ball around his back to an older teammate, who made an easy lay-up.

Reggie and Tony laughed harder. Roland Sims shook his head. And Brian felt his face flush with embarrassment.

"Man, I told you," Sims said.

A car horn sounded from the street. Brian saw a station wagon loaded with other ten-year-olds pull up to the curb. The freckle-faced kid and his buddy grabbed their basketballs and waved good-bye to Brian and the others.

"Who were those kids?" Brian asked, taking his books from Tony.

"Dudes said they played on some kiddie team," Roland answered. "Man, they can be on my team any day."

"Maybe Davis oughta ask 'em for ballhandling lessons," Tony said as the three Patriots left the park.

Reggie and Tony laughed, but Brian felt frustrated that the kids handled the ball better than he did.

"That's Hinkle Fieldhouse?" Brian asked.

"Big, huh?" Reggie said.

"And old," Tony added.

It was just before seven o'clock that same evening. Brian and his two Jefferson teammates had left a city bus and crossed Butler University's small and neatly kept campus on Indianapolis' northwest side. Now, the university's huge basketball arena rose into the cold night sky before them, looking to Brian like a giant brick airplane hangar.

"Place seats fifteen thousand," Tony said as they walked across the rapidly filling parking lot.

"They used to play the state finals here," Reggie added, "before they moved 'em downtown to Market Square Arena."

Brian and his two friends met the coaches and the other Patriots outside Gate E.

"Here are your tickets," Coach Ford said, handing them to the players. "Stay together at half time and after the game. Coach Williams'll give you a tour of the fieldhouse."

"As most of you know," Coach Williams added, "they filmed the movie *Hoosiers* here. The place is part of Indiana basketball history."

"Yeah, ancient history," Cisco Vega said.

The players laughed, then followed the coaches through the entrance gate.

"We'll be sitting behind one of the baskets,"

Coach Ford said as they passed some hotdog and
soft drink stands. "That'll give you a chance to see
the court up close, especially Davis, who's never
been here."

"Courts are all the same," Brian said.

"That's true," Coach Williams said, "but the
shooting background is different for each of 'em."

"Yeah, this place is really huge," Reggie said.

"It's so big," LaMont added, "it's like shooting in
the middle of a parking lot. Throws your aim off."

Brian was about to laugh at his teammates'
remarks when they turned a corner and entered
the court area. He looked around and felt his
mouth drop open. He'd seen the Butler fieldhouse
on TV, but nothing prepared him for what he was
looking at now.

The arena resembled a giant airplane hangar.
The arc-shaped ceiling, supported by old fash-
ioned metal girders, rose two hundred feet above
the brightly lighted court. Packed rows of blue,
red, and yellow bleacher seats climbed in layers
on both sides of the court until Brian could barely
see the last of them up near the shadowy rafters.
The court, its outside border and foul lanes
painted blue, seemed small and almost lost in the
middle of the fieldhouse's open spaces.

"Wow," Brian said, "it *is* big."

"And with so much open space," LaMont said,
"it's tough aiming at the baskets. Even for a
hotshot like you, Davis."

While the last of the sellout crowd filed into the
arena, Brian and his teammates settled into their
front seats behind one of the baskets. The Butler

University band, sitting in the balcony at the other end of the court, played the Butler War Song as their team ran onto the floor. Ohio State followed the Butler Bulldogs, and twenty minutes later the game began.

The first half was exciting and close. Brian and the Patriots enjoyed watching college-level action for a change. At the half time break, Butler led 50–47.

"Man, those dudes are good," Reggie said, as the teams trotted off the court.

"If you think those college guys were something," Coach Ford said, pointing at a team of ten-year-olds racing onto the court, "wait until you see these kids do their stuff."

The big crowd cheered and applauded.

"Hey, a half time show," Tony said.

"Yeah, and look who's with 'em, Davis," Reggie said, pointing.

Brian looked at the twelve kids racing onto the floor. All of them were dressed in white jerseys and red-white-and-blue shorts, and each was spinning a basketball on his right index finger. The freckle-faced kid Brian had played against that afternoon and his stocky friend were leading the group.

"Ladies and Gentlemen," said the PA announcer over the loudspeaker, "Butler University is proud to present for your half time enjoyment, the world famous ball-handling exhibition team, Indiana's own Mighty Mites."

"No wonder those kids in the playground were so good," Brian said.

"Yeah, they're almost professionals," Tony said.

"These kids travel to Europe and Asia every summer to give dribbling exhibitions," Coach Ford said. "I want you guys to watch what good ball handling looks like."

While the big crowd cheered, the Mighty Mites tricky dribbled all over the court and passed their basketballs around their backs, through their legs, and down their arms. They spun their official-sized balls on all ten fingers and even on their elbows, then dribbled down the length of the court while passing their ball between their legs from one hand to the other.

The crowd cheered the Mites' tricks.

"Man, these dudes are great," Reggie said.

"How do they do it?" Terry asked.

"Practice, baby, practice," Coach Williams said.

The Mighty Mites finished with a spectacular dribbling exhibition by the freckle-faced kid Brian had played against. The kid tricky dribbled all over one half-court area while five other Mites players tried to steal the ball from him. The freckle-faced kid passed the ball between his legs, around his back, and through the open legs of the kids who were chasing him. He kept the others from stealing his ball for over a minute and received a standing ovation from the Patriots and the rest of the sellout crowd.

"We need to dribble like that against the press," LaMont said, applauding with everybody else.

"The Mites' coach, Bobby Gutheridge, teaches PE here at Butler," Coach Ford said as the applause faded and the ten-year-olds ran off the court. "He was my college roommate and says he'd like to help us out with some drills."

"Dude was one of the best ball handlers I ever saw," Coach Williams added in his deep voice.

"He's invited us to the locker room after the game," Coach Ford said.

The second half of the Butler-Ohio State game was as exciting as the first. The more experienced Buckeyes used a full-court zone press and finally overcame Butler, 95–82.

After the game, Brian and the Patriots followed Coach Ford down a long ramp to the locker rooms deep in the fieldhouse's basement. They shook hands with some of the dejected Butler players, then met six-foot-five Bobby Gutheridge, coach of the Mighty Mites. Coach Ford's college roommate then pointed at Brian.

"We got some ball-handling drills that oughta help against any press," said the dark-haired Gutheridge, "even for big guys like young Davis."

"We sure need 'em," Brian said.

As the Patriots said goodbye and walked from the fieldhouse into the chilly night, Coach Ford buttoned his coat and stepped over to Brian.

"I've arranged some private ball-handling lessons for you with Bobby," said the coach. "It's the only part of your game that really needs lots of work."

"Thanks, Coach," Brian said.

And, as the players squeezed into the coaches' two cars, Brian pictured himself tricky dribbling like the Mighty Mites.

* * *

Later, at a nearby Hamburger Heaven restaurant, Coach Ford kept his promise and bought burgers and fries for everybody. Brian saw Tony pause long enough for his attack on a double cheeseburger and large fries to point at something in the darkened parking lot.

"Hey, look," Tony said, wiping some ketchup from his mouth with a paper napkin. "It's Hanson."

Brian, Reggie, and Cisco Vega turned in their booth and peered out the steamy window.

"Look at the dudes with him," Reggie said. "Bruce Barrett and his friends."

"Who?" Brian asked, staring at the group of kids.

"Some jerks from Jefferson," Tony said. "All of 'em are troublemakers. They spend more time in Mr. Rhodes's office than they do in class."

"Some dudes at school say Barrett steals exams and sells 'em to other kids," Reggie added.

"You gotta be desperate to buy stolen exams from jerks like them," Tony said. Suddenly he paused with his burger halfway to his mouth and looked at Brian. "You think Hanson is . . . ?"

"Let's hope not," Brian said, getting ready to go after Terry. "That's a sure way to get kicked off the team."

But before Brian and his friends could act, Terry joined the team in the overcrowded Hamburger Heaven.

"Hanson, since when are you and Bruce Barrett friends?" Tony asked. "The guy's bad news."

"We're not," Terry said quickly. He sat in a booth with LaMont and Clarence and looked around at his teammates.. "I . . . I asked him for some history notes, that's all. Is that a crime?"

"Just don't do something stupid, man," LaMont said.

Terry was about to speak, but just then the coaches walked past and hurried the players along. For the sake of the team, Brian hoped Hanson was telling the truth.

FOUR

"Welcome to Jefferson high for tonight's game between the Zellinger Zebras and the Jefferson Patriots."

It was Tuesday evening and Brian and the other Patriots, dressed in their white uniforms, waited impatiently near their bench for the game to start.

"Here is the starting lineup for Zellinger High," Mr. Farnsworth, the PA announcer said.

The Zellinger starters, dressed in purple uniforms, ran onto the court. Brian watched and tried to remember the scouting report the coaches had discussed half an hour ago in the locker room.

"Zellinger's a quick team," Coach Ford had said.

"So watch out for the press," Coach Williams had added.

"Their best players are the Edwards twins," Coach Ford continued. "Edgar and Luther are a couple of six-five black kids who can really sky. And they're fast, too."

"I know the dudes," Clarence Reed said, adjusting his goggles over his eyes. "You gotta block 'em away from the boards or they'll kill us underneath."

"Edgar's your man," Coach Williams said to Brian. "He likes to shoot from the outside, so play up on him."

"You take Luther," Coach Ford told LaMont. "He's quicker than his brother, so cut him off before he drives to the basket."

"Zellinger's only other scoring threat," Coach Ford continued, "is Willie Short, a super-quick six-one black playmaker. He's your man, Dupree. Don't let him drive."

"No sweat," Reggie had said. "I'm psyched."

Now, half an hour later, the game was about to start. Brian and the Jefferson starters were introduced after Zellinger's, and the pep band played the National Anthem.

After some final comments by Coach Ford, the Patriots' usual starting lineup walked to the midcourt circle for the opening jump ball.

The Zellinger Zebras, led by the Edwards twins, walked over to the jump-ball circle and shook hands with Brian and the other Patriots. Edgar Edwards prepared to jump.

"You dudes are gonna lose tonight," Edgar told Brian, a wide grin creasing his black face.

Brian shrugged. "Talk is cheap," he said.

Edgar's face grew serious. "Man, we gonna

stomp all over you. Ain't no way you're a top twenty team."

After checking with the official timer, the ref tossed up the ball between Brian and Edgar Edwards. The six-five Zellinger jumping-jack leaped and easily won the jump, tapping the ball to six-one Willie Short.

"Pick up your men," LaMont shouted. "Play tough 'D'."

Brian turned to run downcourt and Edgar elbowed him in the stomach. He stopped in his tracks, gasping, and tried to catch his breath. Edgar raced toward Zellinger's basket, his right hand raised.

Willie Short passed him the ball for an easy lay-up.

The score: Zellinger 2 and Jefferson 0.

The Zellinger cheerleaders, dressed in purple and white zebra-striped uniforms, yelled and waved pom-poms.

"Man, Davis was fouled," Reggie said to one of the officials. The ref just shrugged.

"Press! Press!" shouted Clarence as he took the ball and prepared to pass it in from out of bounds.

Brian and the other Patriots' starters ran to their positions and set up their press offense. The Zebras quickly formed a two-two-one zone-trap press all over the court.

"Work the play!" LaMont shouted from downcourt.

"Break!" Clarence yelled, slapping the ball.

At Zellinger's free-throw line in front of Reed, Reggie and Terry broke in different directions.

Clarence passed the ball to Reggie, who turned and dribbled along the sideline. Almost immediately, Zellinger's Willie Short and Luther Edwards double-teamed him and made him stop his dribble.

Brian ran across the midcourt line and raised his right hand. "Dupree!" he shouted.

Reggie faked a low bounce pass, then fired a bullet chest pass to Brian just over the ten-second line. He caught the ball and turned to dribble. He was shocked to find Edgar Edwards and Lonnie Daniels, Zellinger's other forward, waiting for him with their arms waving.

Brian tried to stop but dragged his pivot foot. The refs blew their whistles and called him for traveling.

"Let's get it back, homeboy," LaMont said as he ran past Brian.

Brian didn't have time to feel sorry for himself. As soon as Zellinger inbounded the ball, Willie Short passed it to Edgar Edwards on the right side of the foul lane. Brian crouched in a defensive stance and waited for Edgar to make a move. The six-five forward faked once, twice, and then a third time with the ball. Hoping to block the shot, Brian jumped and raised his hands.

Edgar drove easily around Brian for a slam dunk.

The score was now Zellinger 4 and Jefferson 0.

"Watch out for the press!" Coach Ford shouted from the Patriots' bench.

Clarence grabbed the ball and quickly inbounded it to Terry, who began dribbling toward

Jefferson's basket. Willie Short guarded him closely and caused him to dribble off his foot. Luther Edwards picked up the loose ball and laid it in the hoop. Clarence slapped his arm for a foul.

"This stinks," Reggie said, as they lined up on the lane.

"Relax," LaMont told the Patriots. "We're trying too hard."

Luther swished his free-throw, and, before the Zebra rooters stopped cheering, Clarence passed the ball in to Reggie. Zellinger immediately pressed the Patriots. Reggie turned, but, instead of dribbling, he passed the ball the length of the court to LaMont near Jefferson's hoop.

The Patriots' captain caught the ball, pump-faked once, and tried to drive on Lonnie Daniels. But Daniels held his defensive position and LaMont charged into him for a foul.

The Zebra players clapped their hands. With the score 7–0, Coach Ford called time-out.

"Here we go again," Brian said as the Patriots slumped onto their bench. "What's wrong with us, coach?"

"You're so tight, you're playing like rookies," Coach Ford said. "Loosen up a little."

"Coach is right," LaMont said as they walked back onto the court. "We gotta play like we always do. These dudes aren't that tough."

But when play continued, Willie Short faked Reggie out of his socks and drove down the foul lane for a lay-up. LaMont switched from his man and tried to block Willie's shot, but fouled him instead. The basket was good, and the foul was

LaMont's second. Short swished his free throw and Zellinger led 10–0.

Clarence, an angry scowl on his face, quickly grabbed the ball and fired a long pass to LaMont past the midcourt line. Before Zellinger's zone-trap press shifted and smothered them, Brian ran across midcourt and caught a pass from LaMont near the three-point circle.

"Shoot, hotshot!" Edgar shouted as he raced toward Brian.

Brian quickly launched a high-arching twenty-two foot jump shot at the Patriots' basket. Just after he released the ball, he felt Edgar slap him on the wrist for a foul.

The ball swished through the net and Jefferson's rooters exploded with a loud cheer.

"Way to shoot, Davis," Tony shouted from the bench.

"Nice shot, man," Reggie said, bashing forearms with Brian. "Now we're ready to roll."

But after Brian's free throw made the score Zellinger 10 and Jefferson 4, the Zebra's full-court press forced the Patriots to make half a dozen more mistakes. Brian fumbled away one pass and later was called for carrying the ball when he tried to dribble past Edgar. Reggie and Terry threw two wild passes, and Clarence and LaMont each traveled on their way to the hoop.

Late in the quarter, Brian swished another three-point jumper from twenty-five feet. But for most of the first period, the Zebras' press kept the Patriots away from their basket. And at their hoop, Zellinger scored often on easy lay-ups after steals or Patriots' errors.

With ten seconds remaining in the first quarter, LaMont tried to steal the ball from Willie Short and was whistled for his third foul. Coach Ford leaped off the bench to protest, but then was forced to remove the team's captain from the game.

The first quarter ended with the score Zellinger 22 and Jefferson 10.

"Man, you dudes are nothin'," Edgar Edwards said, as he passed Brian on the way to his bench.

Brian didn't reply, but he was almost ready to agree with the Zebras' center.

"You guys are rushing everything," Coach Ford yelled in the team's huddle. Brian toweled off and noticed some panic in the usually calm coach's voice. "Take your time passing and dribbling or Zellinger's gonna blow us outta our own gym."

"Concentrate on your ball handling like you do in practice," Coach Williams added.

The second quarter began with George Ross, a six-two white forward who was in for Jackson and Alvin Woolridge playing Hanson at guard. Brian, Clarence, and Reggie stayed in the game.

But the results were the same.

From the moment Reed inbounded the ball to Dupree and started the quarter, Zellinger pressed the Patriots all over the court. Willie Short stole the ball from Reggie and made a twisting lay-up over Reed's outstretched hand. Then Brian fumbled the ball while dribbling across the midcourt line. Edgar Edwards grabbed the loose ball and started a fast break that ended with a slam dunk by his brother Luther. And on Jefferson's next two plays, the officials whistled Alvin for carrying the ball twice in a row.

To make things worse, when the Patriots were fouled during the Zebras' clinging press, they missed their free throws. Except for Brian, who swished two of three foul shots, the Patriots made only five of fourteen free-throw tries in the half.

On defense, the Patriots couldn't stop the Zebras' many drives to the basket. And they made the situation worse by fouling often. Coach Ford was forced to use Brad Cunningham, Jeff Burgess, and Tony Zarella to finish the second quarter. By the end of the first half, Brian and Clarence had three fouls apiece and all the Patriots were tired, frustrated, and angry.

The score was Zellinger 45 and Jefferson 26, and, for the second game in a row, the Patriots were behind at half time. But this time it was by a whopping margin.

"Man, I can't believe this," Reggie said as the team trudged into their locker room. He kicked his locker and swore to himself.

"We're playing like freshmen!" Hanson said, punching the flimsy wooden door of the uniform locker.

Brian slumped onto the bench in front of his locker and slammed a towel to the floor.

"It's my fault, guys," Brian said. "I scored only eight points and dribbled and passed like a B-team player."

"Getting angry won't help," Coach Ford said, walking into the locker room.

"Neither will hitting lockers or doors," Coach Williams said, examining the locker Dupree hit.

"Doors and lockers didn't miss all those free-throws," Coach Ford said. "Or let Zellinger drive to the basket for wide-open shots. You played lousy and now you'll have to play better if you want to win. It's as simple as that."

The Patriots sat in silence and listened. Music from the pep band filtered into the locker room.

"Coach's right," LaMont said, toweling off. "We're not playing *our* game."

"Yeah, we're letting those Zellinger dudes run all over us," Reggie said. "We gotta take our time and look for good shots. And man, let's make some free throws."

"Now you're talking sense," Coach Ford said.

"Zellinger used only six guys in the first half," Coach Williams said, "so you *know* they gotta be tired."

"And if the dudes are tired," LaMont said, "they won't press as good in the second half."

"I hope so, because we need some shots closer to the basket," Coach Ford said.

"I can get open under the hoop against those Edwards twins," Brian said. "They're wimps on defense."

"Yeah!" Cisco said, bashing forearms with Brian.

Suddenly, the gloomy locker room became a place of hope and enthusiasm again. The team huddled around Coach Ford.

"We can come back against these guys," the coach said. "Let's show 'em something!"

"Let's go!" the Patriots shouted, and then they ran up the stairs to the gym.

The Patriots' rooters seemed to sense the team's enthusiasm. They cheered wildly as the starters walked onto the court and the pep band filled the gym with loud music.

"Don't foul," LaMont shouted to Brian and Clarence, who had three fouls each, as did La-Mont.

The officials blew their whistles and handed the ball to Clarence out of bounds.

"Press!" shouted Reed, looking out at the Zellinger zone-trap full-court defense. "Run the play!"

"Reed!" Brian shouted, raising his hands for a pass.

Clarence zipped a baseball pass toward midcourt and Brian reached for the ball. Edgar Edwards tried to steal the ball and slammed into him for a foul.

"Yeah, all right!" Hanson shouted.

Reed inbounded the ball again, this time to Reggie, who dribbled over midcourt and called out a play.

Brian saw the Zebras were playing a pressing man-to-man in the half-court area, so he faked and feinted, then cut past a pick by Clarence to the free-throw line.

The officials blew their whistles and pointed at Willie Short, who had smashed into Reed's pick.

"Another foul," Reggie said, bashing forearms with Brian. "It's about time!"

Reed passed the ball inbounds again and Brian noticed Edgar Edwards was upset about the fouls and wasn't playing as tight a defense. Reggie saw it, too, and lofted an alley-oop pass above the Patriots' hoop. Brian caught the ball and slammed it through the basket. Edgar reached up and tried to block the shot, but was too late and fouled Brian.

The Jefferson rooters went wild. Brian went to the free-throw line.

"Way to go, homeboy," Reed said, bashing forearms with Brian. "Now make the foul shots. We need 'em."

Brian swished both free throws, and now the score was Zellinger 45 and Jefferson 29.

"Pick up your men," LaMont shouted above the cheers of the fans. "Let's get the ball back."

The Zebras inbounded the ball, and almost immediately Willie Short turned and charged into Reggie for a foul.

"Way to get position on him, Reg!" Cisco shouted from the bench.

Short slammed the ball on the floor in disgust.

"Technical foul, technical foul," yelled the Jefferson rooters.

Clarence inbounded the ball, then set a solid pick against Edgar Edwards. Brian cut to the free-throw line for a pass from Hanson, and turned to shoot a fifteen-foot jumper, but missed. Reed grabbed the rebound and dunked the ball through the hoop. Luther slapped him on the arm for Zellinger's fourth foul in less than two minutes.

The Jefferson rooters stood and cheered. The Zellinger coach yelled at the officials.

But then, Reed missed his free throw, making the score Zellinger 45 and the Patriots 31.

"We're coming back," Hanson shouted.

"Yeah, let's put it to these dudes," Reggie added.

Midway through the quarter, Willie Short and Edgar Edwards each fouled for the fourth time and left the game. A minute later, the officials whistled a fourth foul on Luther Edwards and he also went to the bench. With inexperienced subs in the game, Zellinger switched from a full press to a half-court zone defense.

"Their subs are weak," Coach Ford said during a time-out, "so look for Jackson and Davis near the hoop or Dupree on the wing. Now's our chance to get back in the game."

But when the game continued, LaMont tried to steal a pass and smashed into one of Zebras' subs. And on offense, the Patriots' captain faked a jump shot and charged into his arm. The refs blew their whistles and LaMont fouled out with more than a quarter left to play.

Brian saw the glum expressions on the faces of his teammates, but LaMont clapped and cheered them on.

"You can do it without me," Jackson said. "Keep the comeback going."

With their captain out of the game, the Patriots looked to Brian for points as well as leadership. But Zellinger knew about Brian's scoring ability and double-teamed him under the hoop. Hanson, Dupree, and the others couldn't pass him the ball so they began taking shots of their own.

And Brian became a fierce rebounder.

As the third quarter was ending, Reggie shot a jumper but missed. Brian rebounded the ball, laid it in, and was fouled on the arm. Brain swished his free throw, and then on defense blocked a Zebra shot.

Terry dribbled down the floor, saw Brian was closely guarded and launched a long jumper from beyond the three-point arc. The missed shot bounced off the rim and Brian blocked out perfectly for a rebound. He tore the loose ball away from two Zebra subs and slam-dunked it through the basket.

For the rest of the quarter, Brian continued his one-man assault on the hoop. But missed free throws by his teammates kept the Patriots from catching up to the Zebras. After three periods, they still trailed Zellinger 64–58.

"We're back in the game!" Coach Ford shouted as Brian and his teammates rested on the bench between quarters.

Brian and the starters began the fourth quarter on the bench. Jeff Burgess was in at center, George Ross and Brad Cunningham played forward, and Tony and Alvin played guard. But, after two minutes of missed shots and mistakes, Coach Ford sent the starters back into the game. LaMont was still out of the game.

Despite their fouls, the Zellinger starters also entered the game. Brian and the Patriots continued taking advantage of the slower defense.

Brian swished an eighteen-foot jumper, Reggie made a ten footer from the baseline, and Clarence slammed through a rebound. With two minutes to play, Jefferson had cut the Zebras' lead to three, 78–75.

Zellinger called time-out, and the Patriots walked to their bench amidst the deafening cheers of their rooters.

"Way to go, guys!" LaMont shouted. He bashed forearms with the starters as they sat on the bench.

When the time-out ended and Coach Ford sent the Patriots onto the court, Edgar Edwards walked over to Brian. The six-five center's uniform was soaked to a dark purple with sweat.

Zellinger inbounded the ball and Short tried to sneak a lob pass to Edwards under the hoop. But Brian leaped as high as he could and batted the pass to the side of the basket, where Reggie grabbed it and dribbled downcourt.

After faking and feinting near the Jefferson basket, Brian received a pass from Terry but was double-teamed by the Edwards twins. He faked a shot and passed to Reed, who was fouled by Lonnie Daniels under the basket. It was Daniels' fourth foul.

Reed stepped up to the free-throw line.

"See the basket, see the ball, come on Clarence make 'em!" shouted the Patriots' cheerleaders.

"Take your time and bend your knees," Brian told Reed before the ref handed Clarence the ball.

Reed took the ball, adjusted his goggles, and missed both free throws.

Luther Edwards rebounded for the Zebras and started a fast break in the other direction. Clarence, upset with himself for missing the foul shots, was slow getting back on defense. Luther received a pass near the basket and slam-dunked the ball over Ross, who was in for LaMont.

With just over a minute to play, the score was Zellinger 80 and Jefferson 75.

Suddenly, the Zebras returned to their full-court, zone-trap press. The Patriots were caught by surprise.

Reed tried to pass to Reggie, but Willie Short stole the ball and laid it in. Zellinger led 82–75.

"Work the play," LaMont shouted from the bench.

Reed grabbed the ball and fired a bullet pass to Brian at midcourt. Holding the ball over his head, Davis pivoted into a double-team by Edwards and Short, then heaved a length-of-the-court pass to Reggie. As the Zebras' zone press chased the ball, Brian sprinted alone toward the Patriots' basket and raised his hands.

"Dupree!" Brian shouted as he ran down the foul lane.

Reggie faked a shot and zipped a chest pass to Brian, who slam-dunked the ball and was fouled by Daniels.

The crowd stood and went wild, and Daniels was whistled out of the game with five fouls. After Brian swished a free throw, the score was Zellinger 82 and Jefferson 78.

"Press 'em!" Brian shouted to his teammates.

Reggie stole the inbounds pass from Luther before the Zebras realized what was happening and made a lay-up to make the score 82–80. The rooters from both schools stood and went crazy. Only forty-five seconds was left.

Zellinger didn't call time-out, but instead Luther tossed a floating hook pass to Short at midcourt.

Brian leaped and intercepted the pass.

The Patriots' rooters nearly raised the roof of the gym with a deafening cheer, and Brian's teammates raced downcourt. Reggie was suddenly free near the basket and Brian fired a perfect chest pass, which Reggie grabbed and laid into the loop. The score was tied, 82–82.

"What a comeback!" Terry shouted, bashing forearms with Reggie and Brian.

The Zebras called time-out with thirty-two seconds left to play.

The Jefferson subs rushed onto the court to welcome Brian and the others back to the bench. Then the Patriots huddled around their coaches.

"We gotta steal the ball," Coach Ford shouted over the noise in the gym, "but we can't foul to do it." He looked at Brian. "Davis, I figure they'll work the ball into Edgar near the foul lane, so be ready for it."

"And if we stop those dudes from scoring," Coach Williams said, "look for Davis down at our end."

The buzzer sounded, ending the time-out. As Brian walked onto the court, he felt a ripple of nervousness in his stomach.

"Break that tie! Break that tie!" shouted the several hundred Zellinger rooters.

"De-fense! De-fense!" roared Jefferson's two thousand fans.

Luther Edwards passed the ball to Willie Short and the Zebras set up their half-court offense against the Patriots' man-to-man defense. Less than thirty seconds were left.

The noise in the gym was deafening and Brian couldn't hear his teammates talking on defense. He remembered Coach Ford's advice and played close to Edgar Edwards.

Nineteen seconds remained in the game.

With patience and ball-handling skill, the Zebras froze the ball until only seven seconds were left to play. Then Willie Short tried to lob a pass to Edgar Edwards near the hoop—but Brian reached up and stole the ball.

The fans cheered, and Brian dribbled down-court.

"Davis!" shouted Reggie, raising his hand and racing unguarded toward the Patriots' basket.

But Brian needed to watch the ball to control his dribble and didn't see Reggie—or Clarence, who was standing alone ten feet from the Patriots' hoop.

He didn't see Willie Short, either.

The Zebras' speedy guard sneaked up behind Brian and stole the ball thirty feet from Zellinger's basket.

Brian heard a gasp from the Jefferson rooters.

The seconds ticked away: 0:05, 0:04, 0:03.

Brian stopped and chased after Short. But the six-one guard was already heaving the ball toward his hoop.

As Brian watched and the fans stopped cheering, the ball swished through the net and the final buzzer sounded ending the game. Brian felt his heart sink.

The final score was Zellinger 85 and Jefferson 82.

Zellinger's fans ran onto the court and mobbed Short and the other Zebras. Brian and the Patriots stared at the final score as though they couldn't believe it.

"I lost the game," Brian said later in the Patriots' quiet locker room. "It's all my fault. I shoulda passed the ball."

"It wasn't anybody's fault," Coach Ford said. "Everybody messed up tonight."

"I guess it wasn't our night to win," Coach Williams added.

Despite the kind words, and despite his forty points and nineteen rebounds, Brian knew the Patriots were going to fall from the top twenty ranking because he couldn't dribble without watching the ball.

FIVE

Brian sat staring at his breakfast. His appetite had disappeared after the loss to Zellinger the night before.

"You better eat something," his mom said from across the table.

Helen Davis was a small, pretty woman who was still happy and caring despite the separation from Brian's alcoholic father. Now Brian noticed the concerned expression on her face.

"I'll be all right," he said, pushing away his plate. "Food tastes bad after a tough loss."

"Nobody likes losing," his aunt said, clearing away his plate. She looked like his mom, only taller and with graying hair. "But life goes on, even for ball players."

Brian put on his parka and a knit cap.

"I lost the game last night," he said, picking up his school books. "I let everybody down."

"Oh hush," Aunt Margaret said. "How many games have you won for the Patriots this year?"

"Folks only remember your last game," Brian said, feeling as low as he had ever felt during a basketball season.

"Keep smiling, son," his mom said as she got ready to leave for work. She stood on her tiptoes and kissed him on the cheek. "The season's not over yet."

"The way I've been handling the ball lately," Brian said, heading for the front door, "I wish it were."

Brian joined Reggie and Tony on the sidewalk, and the three teammates trudged through the cold toward Jefferson High six blocks away.

"You see this morning's paper?" Tony asked Brian.

"Naw, I hate bad news first thing in the morning," Brian said, blowing on his hands to warm them.

"Man, they dropped us outta the top twenty," Reggie said, pulling his knit cap over his ears.

"What do you expect for a team with a center who can't dribble?" Brian said bitterly.

They walked the rest of the way to school in silence.

The day at Jefferson High passed slowly and quietly for Brian and the other Patriots. Everybody seemed to know the players were feeling low following the loss to Zellinger and left them

alone. Even Mr. Rhodes, who usually had something to say, avoided the suffering Patriots.

After school, the locker room was quiet as the
players changed into their practice gear. The other
team members seemed afraid to approach Brian
following what had happened at the end of the
game, and their silence made him feel even worse.

"Now I know how losing teams feel," Tony said
finally.

"Yeah, bad," Reggie said, pulling on his practice
jersey.

"We gotta play better, that's all," LaMont said,
lacing up his high-tops. "We're making too many
mistakes."

Terry slammed his locker door and the other
players looked up. Brian had never seen the
redhead so upset.

"We gotta pass the ball to guys who know how
to dribble," Terry said, staring at Brian. "A playmaker would've made the play at the end of last
night's game."

Silence filled the locker room.

"Cool it, man," LaMont said.

"Heck no," Terry said. "Brian should've passed
the ball. Coach always says big guys shouldn't
dribble."

"Hey, the dude scored forty points and hauled
down a mess of rebounds," Reggie said, nodding
at Brian.

"Yeah, without Davis we never would've been
close at the end of the game," Tony added.

After a long moment, Terry took a deep breath

and nodded his head slowly. Brian saw the anger drain from Hanson's face.

"Hey, Brian, I'm sorry," Terry said sheepishly. "I . . . I didn't mean it."

Brian accepted a forearm bash from Terry, and the team was together again.

"I'm so upright about exams, I don't know what I'm saying," Hanson said, shaking his head.

"Yeah, but you were right about one thing," Brian said, closing his locker door. "I can't dribble."

"That's okay, Davis," Cisco said playfully. "Coach Mel's drills oughtta take care of that."

Brian made a face. "Thanks, I'm looking forward to 'em," he said, following the others.

In the gym, Coach Ford whistled the players over to the midcourt jumpball circle. Brian expected the sort of harsh lecture his old coach at Paitnville used to give the team after they'd lost two games in a row. But he was surprised to see Coach Ford as cool and calm as ever.

"That was quite a second half comeback last night," Coach Ford said. "I'm proud of you guys."

"Good job," Coach Williams added.

Brian looked around and saw the other Patriots were also surprised by the praise.

"We're still making too many mistakes," Reggie said.

"Don't worry about 'em," Coach Ford said, looking at Dupree for a moment. "That's why we have practice."

"A few hours of ball-handling drills oughtta

straighten you dudes out," Coach Williams said with a deep laugh.

The players groaned.

"But since you've been practicing pretty hard lately," Coach Ford said, smiling, "I think we'll do something different today. Something I think you'll like."

"A three-point shooting contest," the coach said.

Again, the players just shuffled their feet and didn't show any enthusiasm. Two losses in a row and the pressure of exams were taking the fun out of practice.

"Here's how it works." Coach Ford said, grabbing a ball from a nearby portable rack. "You guys pick somebody to shoot, and if he makes a shot from behind the center line, that'll be the end of today's practice."

Brian saw his teammates' eyes light up.

"Say what?" Reggie said, smiling broadly.

"It's a deal, coach," Terry said.

LaMont took the ball from Coach Ford and handed it to Brian. "Make the shot, man," said the team's captain.

"What if Davis misses?" Tony asked.

Coach Ford smiled. "Then all of you run twenty-five laps and work with Coach Williams for a while."

Brian heard his teammates grumble, but he noticed their enthusiasm had returned for the moment.

"Make the shot, Davis," Cisco yelled.

"Save us, man," Clarence said.

Brian smiled and walked beyond the midcourt line. He turned and faced the basket over forty feet away.

"You dudes might as well starting running laps," Coach Williams said, laughing. "He's gonna miss."

"No way," Alvin said.

"Head for the locker room, guys," Brian said, eyeing the distant hoop. "This is a piece of cake."

The gym grew silent. The players and coaches watched as Brian bent his legs and launched a high-arcing forty-five-footer.

The ball was halfway to the basket when La-Mont started running toward the locker room. "Yes, yes!" he shouted.

The ball swished through the hoop, barely rippling the cotton cord net.

"All right, Davis!" Cisco yelled, jumping in the air.

The players clapped their hands and followed LaMont downstairs to the locker room.

"Nice shot," Coach Ford told Brian, shaking hands.

"Thanks, but I really needed the work on my ball handling."

"You'll get it," the coach said. "Bobby Gutheridge called to arrange a workout for you tonight at the Butler fieldhouse."

"The Mighty Mites' ball-handling drills?" Brian asked.

Coach Ford nodded. "Seven o'clock," he said. "And listen to the guy."

The Butler fieldhouse seemed even bigger to

Brian when it was empty. He walked past the bleachers and the huge arena smelled of stale popcorn.

"Glad you could come, Brian," Bobby Gutheridge said, shaking hands.

The Butler Bulldogs' varsity had finished its regular practice session on the court. Gutheridge and Brian walked onto the floor. Brian looked up at the high ceiling and once again felt like he was standing in the middle of a giant airplane hangar.

"Thanks for taking the time to help me," Brian said.

"From what your coach told me about your last game, you really need some help with your dribbling."

"I tried to dribble and lost the game," Brian said, looking down at his sneakers. The memory hurt.

"Cheer up, kid," Gutheridge said, slapping Brian on the shoulder. "Nobody's born a dribbler. It takes practice."

Coach Ford's dark-haired college roommate walked to one end of the court. He was bouncing a ball with 'Butler University' stenciled on it, while Brian dribbled the Jefferson High basketball Coach Ford had given him when he made varsity. The patter of the balls echoed in the rafters.

"Let's do some basic dribbling drills," Gutheridge said. "Then, in a couple of days I'll introduce you to the Mighty Mites. You can work out with 'em."

Brian laughed. "Those kids'll make me look bad."

"None of our boys could dribble until we showed 'em how."

"Really? They look like naturals to me."

"They learned the basics of dribbling, and then they practiced every day. That's the key, hard work."

"Nobody works harder at hoops than me," Brian said.

Gutheridge nodded. "I know, that's why I think you'll be dribbling like a playmaker in no time."

Gutheridge, who had the biggest hands Brian had ever seen on a guard, showed him the proper stance for dribblers.

"Tall guys gotta bend over when they dribble," Coach Ford's roomie said, demonstrating. "Then dribble low. That gives the defense less of a chance to reach in for a steal."

Brian tried the stance and nodded. "I could've used this in last night's game. The Zellinger kid just reached in and picked me clean. Guess I was dribbling too high."

"And keep your head up," Gutheridge said, showing Brian how to do it. "Don't look at the ball."

Brian smiled and tried to dribble without watching the ball. But then he dribbled it off his foot.

"That happens all the time," Brian said, tracking down his ball.

"That's okay," Gutheridge said, dribbling rapidly in place and watching Brian at the same time. "Soon you'll be able to look up and forget about the ball."

For the next ten minutes, Brian and Gutheridge used the basics and dribbled up and down the court.

"Pick a spot on the wall and watch it while you're dribbling," Gutheridge told Brian over the noise of the bouncing balls. "That'll keep you from looking at the ball."

Brian crouched, and for the first time in his basketball career, dribbled without watching the ball.

"That's it," Bobby Gutheridge shouted.

As he dribbled from one end of the court to the other, dribbling low and staring at a spot on the wall, Brian promised himself never to let another opponent sneak up behind him and steal the ball.

"Keep the fingers of your dribbling hand spread," Gutheridge said. "You can control the ball better."

Finally, after an hour of dribbling practice, Gutheridge smiled at Brian and stopped the workout.

"How do you feel?" the dark-haired coach asked.

"Like a playmaker," Brian said with a smile. He wiped the sweat from his face with a towel.

Twenty minutes later, Bobby Gutheridge stopped his car in front of Brad Cunningham's house and Brian got out.

"You handled the ball well tonight," Gutheridge said before Brian closed the door.

"Thanks, I learned a lot."

"I'll tell the Mites to expect you for Thursday night's practice. Meanwhile, practice what we worked on."

Brian nodded and closed the car door.

After Gutheridge drove away, Brian knocked on the Cunningham's front door and Brad let him in. Reggie was seated at the dining room table with algebra books and sheets of scrap paper spread all around him. He looked tired, and Brian smiled.

"Don't say nothing, Davis," Reggie said, flexing his cramped writing hand. "Cunningham's meaner than my teachers at school. Man, we been at this stuff for two hours."

"Only forty hours more and you'll be ready for your exam," Brad said, playfully.

Brian laughed, then said, "You guys seen Hanson?"

Brad adjusted his thick-lensed glasses. "Wasn't he supposed to study at your place after practice?"

"Yeah, but he never showed."

"Sounds bad," Reggie said, closing his math book.

"Maybe he just forgot," Brad suggested.

"I'll check his place on my way home," Brian said, as he walked to the front door. "It's only two blocks away."

"I'm comin' along, bro," Reggie said, jumping to his feet near the dining room table. "I need a break."

"Me, too," Brad said, reaching for his coat. "Teaching algebra to Dupree is a strain on my brain."

Five minutes later, they were standing on the front stoop of Terry's gray, two-story house. Brian knocked on the front door and heard footsteps approaching from inside the house.

Hanson opened the door and blinked at them.

"What happened to study hall at my place?" Brian asked, blowing on his hands to warm them.

"Wh . . . what?" Terry said, confused.

"You know, U.S. History, your favorite subject," Brad said, adjusting his glasses and smiling.

"Yeah, Hanson, the course you gotta pass if you want to keep playing ball," Reggie added.

"Oh yeah," Terry said, looking down at his feet and then up at his teammates. "Um, look, Brian . . . I'm feeling kinda sick tonight. Must be the flu or something."

"You looked okay at practice," Brad said.

"I . . . got sick after I got home," Terry said, touching his midsection. "Must be the stomach flu."

Brian stared at Terry. "What about history?"

"I'm reading it now," Terry said, looking from one teammate to the other. "Really, I am. I'm gonna pass the exam, don't worry." He tried to smile, but couldn't.

Brian paused, then said, "You still talking to Bruce Barrett and his crowd?"

"No," Terry said quickly. Then his face became as red as his hair and his green eyes flashed with anger. "What if I was? That's none of your business, Davis."

"Man, anything to do with the team is our

business," Reggie said. "We don't want to lose a playmaker."

"Yeah, and anybody hanging out with Barrett and those jerks is asking for trouble," Brad said.

Brian watched as Hanson's anger faded and he looked down at his feet.

"I . . . I told you, I'm sick," Terry said.

"Bro, you gonna be even sicker if you can't play ball," Reggie said.

Terry looked at each of them, then slammed the door.

"Dude's got a problem," Reggie said as they walked toward the street.

"Maybe it's the team's problem, too," Brian said.

The three of them walked away in silence.

SIX

After leaving Terry's house, Brad and Reggie returned to their study hall and Brian walked home. He spent an hour doing his homework, then Tony stopped by and they practiced hoops at the basket attached to the garage out back. A dim street lamp lighted the driveway.

"Keep your head up when you dribble," Brian said.

"I know," Tony said, shooting a jump shot. "It's you big guys who gotta learn that stuff."

"Yeah, well, the way to learn it is to pick a spot on a wall and watch it while you're dribbling," Brian said, demonstrating the technique. The ball bounced off his foot.

Tony chuckled. "Way to go, Davis," he said.

"It takes practice, that's all."

"Gutheridge show you any other cool moves?"

"Yeah, to keep my body bent over when I dribble," Brian said, crouching as he bounced the ball.

"That's no trick," Tony said, dribbling all over the driveway, "that's just how you do it."

They spent fifteen minutes practicing ball handling. Zarella tried to steal the ball from Brian, but couldn't.

"Not bad, homeboy," Tony said. "Keep it up and Coach Ford'll make you a playmaker."

"That's cool, but all I want is to beat the full-court presses the other teams keep throwing at us," Brian said.

As they shot for a few minutes, blowing on their hands to warm them, Brian told Tony about Hanson.

"You think Hanson told the truth tonight?" he asked. "The guy's never been sick since I known him."

Brian wiped his face and shook his head. "Terry sure looked strung out about something," he said. "Maybe he really is talking with Barrett about stolen exams."

Brian dribbled around the driveway. Finally, he stopped and looked at Tony.

"If he is, and gets caught, we could lose our starting playmaker."

Tony shot a jumper. "That's all we need after losing two games in a row and dropping outta the ratings."

"But Hanson wouldn't do it," Brian said. "He's not dumb."

"No, but he's flunking history, and when you're a senior, that ain't too cool."

Brian nodded glumly, then swished a jumper.

They shot baskets in silence for another ten minutes. Brian was thinking about the team's troubles when suddenly Reggie and Brad walked briskly down the driveway and joined them. Brian noticed their worried expressions.

"Hanson's in trouble," Reggie said, stepping over to Brian. His breath was steamed in the cold night air.

"We gotta save him," Brad added.

Brian and Tony stopped shooting baskets.

"What are you guys talking about?" Tony asked, wiping sweat from his stubbled face.

"Hanson's gonna buy a stolen history exam from Bruce Barrett tonight," Brad said.

The bad news struck Brian like a rebounder's elbow to his head. "You sure?" he asked, suddenly worried.

"Wow, how'd you find out?" Tony asked.

"Danny Warren, a dude from my neighborhood," Reggie said, "is pretty tight with Barrett and his jerks."

"We were finishing algebra about ten minutes ago when Warren stopped by my place," Brad said.

"Danny said Hanson's waiting at the Hamburger Heaven near the park," Reggie said. "Barrett's supposed to drop off the exam later."

"You believe what Warren says?" Brian asked, toweling off.

"Yeah, the dude's in tight with a jerk like Barrett," Tony said.

Reggie nodded. "Bro and me grew up together. Danny knows how much the team means to me. When he heard Barrett talking about Hanson's exam, he figured he better tip me off."

"Now we know why Terry didn't want to study tonight," Brian said. "He'd already made a deal with Barrett."

"Yeah, instead of hitting the books, Hanson decided to take a shortcut," Tony said.

"A short cut off the team," Brad said.

"What are we gonna do?" Reggie asked.

Brian looked down at Tony. "Feel like walking to Hamburger Heaven with me?" He said.

"Man, Zarella lives on burgers," Reggie said, smiling.

"This is business," Brian said, "not dinner. Hanson's about to make the mistake of his life and we gotta talk him out of it."

Tony nodded. "Let's go for it."

"We're coming, too," Reggie said, looking at Brad.

Brian shook his head. "You better wait at Brad's in case Warren picks up some more news," he said.

"That's cool," Reggie said. "But let us know what happens with Hanson."

"You'll be the first to know, Dupree," Brian said.

"This is like a TV show," Brad said over his shoulder as he and Reggie walked down the driveway.

"Let's hope it has a happy ending," Brian said.

* * *

Brian and Tony arrived at the Hamburger Heaven a few minutes past ten o'clock. The fast food restaurant was almost empty. Brian saw Hanson sitting in a booth with two boys and all of them were sipping Cokes. They looked up when Brian and Tony walked toward them.

"You know those guys?" Brian quietly asked Tony as they approached the booth.

"Yeah, they're friends of Barrett," Tony said.

"We gotta get rid of 'em if we want to talk with Terry."

They reached the booth and Brian saw a surprised look pass over Terry's face.

"Davis," said the redheaded senior, forcing a smile. "What's up?"

"I was about to ask you the same thing," Brian said. "We can start by talking about next week's history exam."

"And about the basketball team," Tony added. He looked at Barrett's two friends. "How about asking these jerks to leave."

"Get lost," said one of the boys, a curly-haired kid with pimples. His skinny friend seemed ready to fight.

Brian leaned on the table and towered over them.

"That's a good idea," he said, looking from one to the other. "Why don't you boys get lost for a while?"

The kids looked at Brian, then at Terry.

"We'll wait for you outside," the curly-haired kid said finally. They got up and left the restaurant.

"I'm hungry," Tony said, walking toward the cash registers to place an order. "Be right back."

Brian slid into the booth, knocking his knees against the cramped table. He looked around and then over at Terry, who seemed nervous.

"You crazy or something?" Brian asked softly.

"Wha . . . what do you mean?" Terry said, sipping his Coke.

"Look, we know all about your deal with Barrett. Buying a stolen exam is asking for trouble."

Terry shook his head. "Man, Barrett said nobody would find out," he said, chewing some ice from his drink.

"Everybody'll find out if you go through with this," Brian said. "Especially Coach Ford and Mr. Rhodes."

Terry continued to sip his Coke and look at the table.

"Besides, the team needs you."

Terry continued to stare at the tabletop.

"Also, you're like the rest of us. You need hoops or you'll go bananas," Brian said.

Terry looked up. "I know," he said.

"So why didn't you at least try studying at my place?"

Terry looked at brian, and he saw the desperation in the redhead's eyes. "Look, man, I'm so far behind in history, I figured the only way to save my butt was to make a deal with Barrett."

"Yeah, well you figured wrong," Brian said. "Even if you get a copy of the exam, you gotta look it over and then study the answers. Seems like lots of extra work to me."

"I . . . I didn't think about that," Terry said.

"Besides," Brian added with a smile, "at my place you could've pigged out on my aunt's chocolate chip cookies. Zarella swears they're the best."

Terry laughed for the first time, and Brian knew his heart-to-heart talk was affecting his teammate.

"Zarella never saw a chocolate chip cookie he didn't like," Hanson said.

They both laughed, until Tony rushed over to them.

"Look out the window," Tony said, putting down a tray of burgers and fries. "It's Dupree and Brad Cunningham."

Brian turned in the booth and saw Reggie and Brad dashing into the restaurant.

"There's . . . police cars . . . and TV vans . . . down at . . . the school," Reggie said between gasps.

Brian figured they must have sprinted across the park to the Hamburger Heaven.

"Police cars?" Tony said, nibbling on a fry.

"Dupree, what are you talking about?" Brian asked.

Brad controlled his panting, and looked first at Terry and then at Brian.

"Danny Warren came back to my place ten minutes ago," Brad said, adjusting his thick-lensed glasses.

"Dude said somebody told the cops Barrett was stealing exams down at school tonight," Reggie said.

Everybody looked at Terry, who blushed with embarrassment and bowed his head.

"I . . . I was supposed to get the stolen history final from Barrett tonight," Terry said softly. "He and some of his friends were gonna bust into school tonight, then meet me and some other kids here. We were gonna pay him."

Brian and the others were quiet for a moment.

"Man, let's get over to the school," Reggie said, rushing toward the door.

Brian and the others followed without another word. Tony grabbed a cheeseburger off his tray, then ran after them.

They sprinted four blocks through the chilly night until finally they saw the flashing strobe lights atop the police cars. Brian also saw two TV news vans parked near Jefferson High's main entrance.

The small group of Patriots stopped on the sidewalk across the street. Panting heavily, they watched as several police officers escorted Barrett and two of his buddies, all of them handcuffed, to the cars.

"Wow, this really is like TV," Brad said.

"Yeah, and the bad guys got caught again," Tony added.

As the night air cooled the sweat on his face, Brian watched the policemen help Barrett and the two other kids into the back seats of different police cars.

Brian looked at Terry and saw the color draining from the redhead's face.

"That could've been me," Terry said softly.

The other Patriots turned and stared at Hanson.

"Say what?" Reggie said.

"Barrett asked me to go along tonight," Terry explained, looking at his teammates. "I . . . I almost went."

Brad made a whistling sound and shook his head.

"I can't believe how stupid I've been," Terry said, watching as the police cars with the three handcuffed kids in the backseats drove away.

"I can," Brian said. "Now you gotta hit the history books."

"Yeah, our playmaker's gotta pass his exam," Tony said.

SEVEN

"So, Barrett was stealing exams, huh?"

"Yeah, they finally caught him."

"I wonder who was going to buy the tests."

The break-in was the main topic of discussion at Jefferson High on Thursday, which was fine with Brian since it drew attention away from the varsity's losing streak and Hanson's problem.

Only the varsity players knew about Hanson's connection with Barrett. They discussed it with Terry in the locker room as they dressed for practice.

"That was a dumb thing to do, Hanson," Tony said, as he pulled on his practice jersey.

"Yeah, you risked everything for a jerk like Barrett," Cisco added.

"Man, no way I would've used a stolen exam," Reed said. "Better to flunk the test than go to jail."

"Or get booted outta school," Woolridge added.

Brian watched as Terry just nodded glumly and continued changing into his practice gear. The redheaded senior still looked scared after what had happened the night before.

"Hanson made a mistake," LaMont said, shutting his locker door. "Now, we gotta decide whether the dude should tell Coach Ford about it."

Brian watched as Terry looked up quickly.

"No way," he said, glancing from one teammate to another. "He'd kick me off the team. Maybe even outta school, like Woolridge said."

"We're a team," Reed said, pulling his goggles over his eyes. "We win together and we lose together."

"And we tell Coach the truth," Brian added.

The locker room fell silent for a moment. All eyes stared at Hanson.

"It's the righteous thing to do, man," Jackson added.

Hanson looked up, fear still in his eyes, then nodded.

"All right!" Cisco said, bashing forearms with Terry.

"Coach'll understand," Tony said, walking up the stairs leading to the gym.

"I hope so," Terry said fearfully.

The Patriots shot baskets for ten minutes before Coach Ford blew his whistle and called them together at midcourt.

"I hope you enjoyed your day off from practice," the coach said. "Now, it's back to work."

"We travel to Jackson's gym tomorrow night," Coach Williams added. "Let's get back on the winning track."

"All right!" Reggie said, bashing forearms with Cisco.

"But first," Coach Ford said, looking at Terry, "LaMont told me Hanson has something to say."

The team looked at Terry, and Brian saw Hanson's face go white.

"Man, tell him," Reed said gently.

An edgy silence filled the gym.

"I . . . I was going to buy a stolen history exam from those guys who got busted here last night," Terry finally blurted out. "I . . . I know it was wrong, Coach, and I'd like to apologize to you and the team." Terry looked down at his sneakers. "I think I've learned my lesson."

Silence again.

"I'm glad you told me, Terry," Coach Ford said, "even though what you were about to do was wrong."

"There's no room for cheaters on this team," Coach Williams said in his deep voice. "Or in this school, either."

"What are you going to do, Coach?" Terry asked, looking up at Coach Ford.

"How about this," the young coach said, stroking his chin. "Hanson's always been a solid member of this team, so I'll leave his punishment, if any, up to the rest of you guys. That's fair, especially since Hanson's suspension from school would've hurt the team's chances."

LaMont stepped forward. "What bro did about

the exams was bad," the team's captain said. "But his biggest mistake was forgetting about the team."

"Man, if he'd been suspended, it would've left us without an experienced playmaker for the rest of the season," Reggie added.

Brian and the other Patriots nodded.

"Yeah, and the state tourney's only two weeks away," Tony said.

"Coach, I think we oughtta let Hanson practice," LaMont said, "but he's gotta sit out our next game. That'll be punishment enough, right guys?"

"Yeah, a one-game suspension and all the history books he can read," Tony said, bashing forearms with Cisco.

The team laughed, and Terry looked relieved.

"Don't worry, studying history beats sitting in the back seat of a police car," Terry said, smiling finally.

The players clapped and cheered playfully.

Coach Williams came out from the coach's office pushing a portable metal table with a VCR and a TV on it. He inserted a video tape and the screen flashed to life, showing several pro basketball stars dribbling during some long-ago games.

"Here are half a dozen of the best ball handlers in the history of basketball," Coach Ford said.

"Hey, there's Pistol Pete Maravich," Tony said.

"Yeah, and Mark Jackson of the Knicks," Cisco added. "What's he doing there with those old-timers?"

Coach Williams pointed at the screen, and Brian

saw a small white guard in a Boston Celtics uniform dribbling fast.

"Bob Cousy," Brian said, remembering some old films he saw once. "Played with Boston back in the fifties and sixties."

Coach Williams nodded. "That dude could really handle the ball," he said. "Watch this."

On the screen, Cousy dribbled behind his back and threw a behind-the-neck pass to former Celtic great Bill Russell, who dunked the ball.

"Watch those dribblers closely," Coach Ford said, "and you'll see how they use their ball-handling skills to get away from the defense."

"Look, it's Magic Johnson," Terry said, pointing at the TV. "And John Stockton."

Brian and the other Patriots watched the tape for several minutes. It was like watching a basketball clinic.

"Any questions?" Coach Williams asked as he turned off the VCR.

The Patriots shook their heads.

"Great," Coach Ford said, "now let's get to work. Right, Coach?"

Coach Williams smiled.

"Right. I want four groups of three players each for the zigzag dribbling drill," said the heavyset assistant coach.

"Our ball handling has cost us two losses already," Coach Ford said, "so work hard on these drills."

Brian and his teammates each grabbed a ball and practiced dribbling for ten feet at an angle to the left. Then, after crossing over with the ball, they dribbled ten feet at an angle to the right, continuing in a zigzag pattern all the way down-court.

"Way to go, homeboy," LaMont said to Davis as they passed during the zigzag drill. "You're looking good."

"Bring on the press," Brian said. "I'm ready."

Fifteen minutes later, Coach Williams blew his whistle.

"Okay, put some chairs on the court. Let's see who can dribble around 'em without losing his ball."

"Piece of cake," Brian said a few minutes later. He crouched and dribbled easily around the row of metal folding chairs.

"Man, homeboy's feeling it today," Reggie said.

The dribble continued for ten minutes.

"That's better, Davis," Coach Ford said. "Now, maybe we'll be able to get past those trapping presses."

Next, Brian and the other Patriots were surprised when the coaches brought a dozen B-team players into the gym.

"Okay, listen up," Coach Williams said. "You varsity types are gonna run the press offense against these B-team guys." The heavy-set coach stoked his goatee and smiled. "Think you hotshots can handle it?" he added.

"No sweat," Reggie said, "but seven of 'em?"

"Just think about it, Dupree," Coach Ford said. "If you can beat the full-court press by seven guys in practice, it oughta be easy to get past five guys during a game."

Brian and the other Patriots exchanged glances, then nodded.

"Coach's right," Jackson said. "Let's do it."

The Patriots' starting five clapped their hands, then took their places on the court. The B-team players, nervousness showing on their young faces, set up a full-court man-to-man press against the starters.

"Let's put it to 'em," Cisco yelled from the sidelines.

"Yeah, blitz 'em," Tony added.

Reed took the ball out of bounds and slapped it. The varsity starters ran to their positions in the press offense, and Reed snapped a chest past to Dupree. Reggie turned and immediately found himself being guarded by three B-team kids.

"Dupree!" Brian shouted, running across half court.

Reggie faked a return pass to Reed, then fired a bullet pass to Brian near midcourt. Brian leaped and grabbed the ball with both hands, then landed and crouched against the two B-team defenders who were guarding him closely.

When one of the inexperienced defenders reached in for a steal, Brian pivoted away and began to bounce the ball. Dribbling with his head up, Brian quickly spotted LaMont free under the hoop and passed him the ball for an unguarded lay-up.

"Way to go, Davis!" shouted Coach Williams.

"Run the play again," Coach Ford said.

Reggie and Tony bashed forearms with Brian, who smiled, and for the first time in weeks, felt pleased with his ball handling.

EIGHT

Bobby Gutheridge smiled as he drove his Honda Civic across town. He looked at Brian sitting beside him.

"So, you remember Bob Cousy?"

"Only from some old films on TV," Brian said.

Gutheridge chuckled. "The 'Cooz' was the greatest ballhandler of all time."

It was Thursday night after supper. Gutheridge had just picked up Brian at his aunt's house and was taking him to a Might Mites' practice. After studying the War of 1812 with Hanson after practice, Brian was ready to learn some of the Mites' ball-handling tricks.

"Cousy was doing his magic before Earvin Johnson was even born," Gutheridge added.

"He sure liked to dribble around his back," Brian said.

Gutheridge nodded, then looked at Brian. "Hold up your hands," he said. Brian did.

"What is it?" Brian asked.

"Cousy handled the ball so well because he had such big hands," Gutheridge explained.

Brian looked at his own hands. "And mine?"

"Ham sized," Gutheridge said, smiling. "Just what you need for controlling a basketball."

"Yeah, but my legs are too long. Makes for high dribbles. Small guards are stealing me blind."

Gutheridge nodded and drove his car into the parking lot of the northside middle school.

"No problem," he said, parking near the entrance to the school's small gym. "Watch some of the Mites' drills and they'll have you handling a ball smart and tight." Gutheridge laughed and got out of his car.

"I'll settle for not bouncing the ball off my feet." Brian said, as he followed him into the gym.

Inside the gym, the twelve Mighty Mites players were dribbling, spinning, and flipping red-white-and-blue basketballs near all six baskets. Brian was surprised to see half a dozen fathers helping out with the practice. He suddenly wished his dad was there to watch him play, too.

"The fathers help with the drills," Gutheridge said, as if reading Brian's mind. They took off their winter coats. "Come on, I'll introduce you to the gang." He blew the whistle hanging around his neck.

Brian stood awkwardly at midcourt while Bobby Gutheridge introduced him to the team and their dads.

"I saw him on TV," one of the kids said. He was a dark-haired boy who barely came up to Brian's waist.

"Yeah, and I played against him at the park the other day," said the freckle-faced boy who had dribbled circles around Brian.

"Made me look sick, too," Brain said, feeling himself blush a little.

"Of course he did," said the stocky kid who'd also been at the park. "Ricky's a Mighty Mite."

Gutheridge nudged Brian and smiled. "Cocky kid, eh?"

"The Patriots need some of their confidence," Brian said. "It's tough losing two in a row."

The Mites' practice began with dribbling drills like the ones Coach Williams used. As the practice wore on, Brian was surprised when none of the kids shot at the baskets and asked the coach about it.

"We're a ball-handling exhibition team," Gutheridge explained over the patter of the bouncing balls, "so we concentrate on dribbling." He playfully elbowed Brian. "Besides, just about everybody can shoot, Davis."

Brian did the drills with the Mites and felt stupid as he towered over the kids. After ten minutes, Gutheridge blew his whistle.

"Station drills," he shouted.

As the Mites ran to begin another exercise, Gutheridge looked at Brian and said, "Watch 'em now."

The twelve Mighty Mites spread out over the court and stood in place while they practiced behind-the-back and behind-the-neck passes to themselves. They opened the legs and zipped bounce passes from front to back, catching their basketballs with amazing quickness. They passed their balls around their legs, their arms, and their backs, and finished the station drills by spinning their red-white-and-blue balls on each of their ten fingers.

Brian stared at the kids, his mouth open. "Wow," he said finally. "And they're only ten years old."

Gutheridge chuckled, then blew his whistle. "Okay, free dribbling," he shouted. "Practice your moves."

The kids yelled and dribbled around.

"Hey, Brian," said Ricky, the freckle-faced kid. "Wanna try the station drill?"

"Go ahead," Gutheridge said, "it'll be good for you."

"Yeah, good for a laugh," Brian said. He followed Ricky to midcourt and started the tricky routine.

"Watch me," Ricky said, whipping his red-white-and-blue ball around his back and between his legs. "It's easy."

Brian chuckled, then tried the same routine.

He passed his ball around his back from one hand to the other, and lost control. His ball bounced away.

"Open your hands wide," Ricky said, still whipping his ball around various parts of his body.

Brian retrieved his basketball and started again. A few minutes later, he was passing the ball

behind his back like an experienced member of
the Mighty Mites. Feeling more confident, he tried
passing the ball around each leg and behind his
neck. After several embarrassing mistakes, he
finally passed well enough to earn some applause
from the other Mites, who were now watching
him.

"That's the way," said Teddy, the stocky kid.

"Yeah, Davis might even be good enough to join
us," added Louie, the small dark-haired kid.

"Only if he shrinks a little," Ricky said, smiling.

All the Mites laughed, as did their fathers.

"Not bad for a sharpshooting center, Davis,"
Bobby Gutheridge said with a grin. "See, your big
hands really do help your ball handling. Practice
these drills every day."

The Mites' workout included more drills. Brian
continued to enjoy himself.

"Take this," Gutheridge said, handing a stiff
paper plate to Brian and then some more to the
Mites. "It's for our next drill."

"A paper plate?" Brian said, watching as the
Mighty Mites placed the plates in their mouths.

"The plate acts like a blinder," Coach Ford's
six-five college roomie said. "When you hold it
with your teeth, you can't see the ball while you're
dribbling it. It's tough at first, but after a while
your ball handling really improves. And it's something you can do at home, too."

Brian watched the Mites dribble all around the
court, their paper plates clenched between their
teeth. Not once did anyone lose control of his
dribble or look down.

"Try it," Gutheridge said, "and follow me." The dark-haired coach put a plate in his mouth and dribbled away.

"Here goes nothing," Brian said to himself.

He placed the paper plate in his mouth and began dribbling toward the far end of the gym. He felt blind and almost immediately bounced the ball off his right foot.

"Practice the drill standing in place at first," Ricky said, taking his plate from his mouth. "It's easier to find the ball that way. Then later you can start moving around."

"Thanks."

Ricky was right, and after a few minutes of practice, Brian found he could dribble well with the paper plate clenched between his teeth. He then moved around the court and was surprised to find himself controlling the bouncing ball without losing it. Finally, he sped up his dribble, practiced crossover moves, and did the zigzag drill—all without fumbling the ball once.

Next, the Mighty Mites put away their paper plates and practiced their famous full court dribbling routines, including full-speed behind-the-back and between-the-legs ball-handling moves. Brian shook his head and looked at Gutheridge.

"No way I can do that stuff," Brian said, "with or without a paper plate in my mouth."

"Take it slow at first," Gutheridge said, joining the Mites on the court, "and let those long arms and big hands of yours do all the work. Just don't watch the ball."

"Come on, Davis," Ricky shouted in his high-pitched ten-year-old's voice. "Show us your moves."

Brian joined the long line of fast-dribbling Mites and dribbled slowly up and down the court. Feeling the stares of all the Mites, he awkwardly tried to bounce the ball behind his back to his other hand. He released the ball too soon and it bounded away, never making it completely around his back.

"Reach all the way around your back with your passing arm," Ricky said as Brian tracked down his ball. "And have your other hand wide open and ready to grab the ball."

Ricky then demonstrated several perfect behind-the-back dribbles, smiling up at Brian when he was finished.

Brian took a deep breath and started again. After several more attempts, he finally completed a behind-the-back dribble pass to himself without muffing the play.

"Way to go, Davis," shouted Teddy, smiling.

Fifteen minutes later, Gutheridge blew his whistle and ended the Mites' practice session.

"Now it's exam time," Gutheridge said as he collected the basketballs from the Mighty Mites. "You and me, one on one, and you gotta use all the moves you just learned."

"Beat him, Davis," Ricky shouted.

"Naw, I betcha a Coke Coach Gutheridge'll kick his butt," Teddy said.

As the Mighty Mites shouted among themselves, Brian and Bobby Gutheridge started their half-court game.

"We'll play to ten baskets," Coach Ford's old roomie said. "If you make a hoop, you keep the ball."

"Let's go," Brian said.

The Mites clapped along the sidelines.

Gutheridge tossed the ball to Brian, who faked a jump shot from the top of the key, rising a little off his feet. Taking advantage of the fake, Brian lowered his head and dribbled toward the hoop. Gutheridge recovered in time to run back and cut him off just before he reached the basket.

Using his newly dribbling moves, Brian quickly made a behind-the-back bounce pass to his left side and dribbled away from Gutheridge for an easy lay-up.

The Mites cheered.

"Fast learner, eh?" the coach said, patting Brian on the back.

"I had some good teachers," Brian said, nodding over at the Mighty Mites.

"You're a great shooter from outside," Gutheridge added as they prepared to play again, "these new dribbling moves oughtta make you tough to guard."

Brian and Gutheridge played for ten minutes. After some early success with his new dribbling moves, Brian realized he needed to practice some more before trying them in a Patriots' game. Gutheridge finally won their one-on-one match 10–8, but Brian was pleased with his ball-handling progress.

"Not bad, Davis," Ricky said as he was leaving the gym with his father. "A few more lessons and you'll be ready to join the Mighty Mites." The freckled-faced kid laughed.

Brian waved good-bye to the Mites as they left.

"Good kids," Gutheridge said as he locked up the middle school's gym and walked to his car.

"Good ball handlers," Brian said, getting into the Honda's front seat.

"Yeah, but it takes more than ball handling to win a championship," Gutheridge said. He started the car. "You need that extra spirit."

"Spirit?" Brian asked, puzzled.

"I'll show you," Gutheridge said, driving onto the main road. "It won't take long."

Five minutes later, they pulled up in front of a white two-story house in a quiet residential neighborhood.

"Larry Meyers lives here," Gutheridge explained as he walked to the front door and rang the doorbell. "He's a retired teacher from Butler and he owns the largest collection of Indiana high school basketball photos and souvenirs in the state. I want to show you something."

Meyers, a slender white-haired man with a cane, opened the door and smiled at them. After Gutheridge introduced Brian, they entered the house and walked down to a basement full of Indiana high school team photos, pennants, old basketballs, scoreboards, and other state tournament mementos. It looked like a museum.

"Look at anything you want," Meyers said in a thin, scratchy voice. He gestured at all the material.

"Here's what I'm looking for," Gutheridge said

right away. He pointed at two old black-and-white team photos in dusty frames on the wall.

"Ah yes," Meyers said, nodding. "The comeback kids."

"Who?" Brian asked, looking at the photos more closely.

"Moore City and Gladden Springs, Indiana State Champs in 1942 and 1956," Gutheridge said, peering at the faded photos. "They're high school legends."

Meyers nodded. "Both schools lost quite a few games at the end of the regular season," he said in his scratchy voice, "but they came back to win the state championship."

"They didn't quit on themselves," Gutheridge said.

"Spirit?" Brian said, looking at Gutheridge.

"That's right, the kind of never-say-die spirit you have at Jefferson High," Gutheridge said, winking at Brian. "There's no way you and the other Patriots should let two losses in a row, or some ball-handling mistakes, get you down."

Brian nodded. It was up to him to get the Patriots' spirit back. And tomorrow night's game was where he'd start.

NINE

"Jackson High," Tony said, peering out one of the team bus's dirty windows. "Look at this place."

"Man, it's like an old prison," Reggie added as they stopped in front of the tiny gym.

"It's the oldest high school in the city," Tony said, shaking his head in disgust. "Look at those old windows and the cracked brick walls."

"We better not lose to a team from a school like this," Cisco said.

"It wouldn't be cool," Terry said as the players stepped off the bus. He was along for the game even though he wouldn't be playing.

It was Friday night and Brian and his teammates were on Indianapolis' north side to play an early February game against the Jackson Runnin' Rebels, one of the city's weakest teams. Only two weeks remained until the state tournament, and the Patriots were eager to end their losing streak and climb back into the top twenty ratings.

Brian and the other Jefferson players walked through the tiny Jackson gym on their way to the locker room.

Brian looked at the several hundred fold-out bleacher seats on each side of the court.

"I've seen bigger elementary school gyms," Brian said.

"Wait until you see the locker room, homeboy," Clarence said. "Man, forget about hot water."

"And look at this warped court," George Ross said.

"It's full of dead spots," Jackson said, looking at Brian. "So be careful when you do those new Mighty Mites moves."

The Patriots laughed and entered the locker room.

His teammates were right, and Brian changed into his blue away uniform in one of the coldest and crummiest locker rooms he'd ever seen. Paint was peeling off the walls, and the locker doors were dented and didn't close properly. The place smelled like old jocks and trainer's balm.

"This place oughta be condemned," Reed said, lacing his high-tops and looking around.

"I think it already is," Cisco said, laughing and bashing forearms with Tony.

"Man, Jackson's team oughtta be condemned, too," Reggie said, pulling on his blue warm-up suit.

"I hear these dudes can't do nothin'," Clarence said, adjusting his goggles over his eyes.

"They'll beat you if you let 'em," Coach Ford

said, as he and Coach Williams walked into the dingy locker room.

"Besides, we've been beating ourselves lately," Coach Williams added. "We gotta handle the ball better."

"Ain't that the truth," Reggie said, sitting on the bench near the lockers. "Man, I'm tired of losing."

"The B-team game is finishing," Coach Ford said, checking his wristwatch, "so let's go over the Jackson scouting report we talked about at practice yesterday."

"Some of these Jackson kids are pretty good," the young head coach said, checking his clipboard.

"Yeah, the two ball boys," Tony said, smiling.

The other Patriots laughed, then settled down when the coach raised his hand.

"Anybody'll beat you if you give 'em a chance," Coach Williams said in his baritone voice. "Don't forget what happened to us during the last two games."

Serious expressions replaced the smiles on the players' faces.

"Davis, what do you know about Jackson's center, Jarvis Poindexter?" Coach Ford asked, looking at Brian.

"He's a six-eight black kid who can't shoot much but likes to hit the boards on missed shots."

"Block the dude away from the basket," Coach Williams added. "And play away from him on defense."

"In fact," Coach Ford said, "Poindexter is so bad a shooter from outside, let him shoot. I want

Davis playing defense in the foul lane to help with everybody else's men."

"Sorta like a one-man zone?" Brian asked.

Coach Ford nodded. "But be sure to put your body on Poindexter when you go for rebounds. The kid *can* jump."

"What about Hoyt Braxton, Dupree?" Coach Ford asked, checking his clipboard again.

"The dude's a slow six-two white kid who likes to put up three-pointers," Reggie said.

"The guy doesn't like pressure, so play up on him," Coach Williams added.

"Man, I'm gonna be inside the boy's high-tops," Reggie said, bashing forearms with Cisco.

"That leaves Kenny Green, Jackson's only other scoring threat," Coach Ford said, looking at La-Mont.

"Dude's a six-three black kid who can't shoot a lick," the Patriots' captain said. "I know Green from the neighborhood. The boy hates pressure, too, so play up on him."

"Hey, looks like none of Jackson's players can shoot," Tony said.

"That's right," Coach Ford said, "so put it to 'em."

"All right!" Cisco shouted, clapping his hands.

"We're due for a big win, guys," Coach Ford continued, trying to pump up the Patriots. "We don't have another game for a week because of exams, so whattya say we do it tonight?"

"Yeah, let's bash 'em!" shouted Ross, bashing forearms with Clarence.

The Patriots all stood and clapped their hands,

then huddled around Coach Ford and touched hands.

"The tournament's just around the corner, guys," the coach said. "Let's show Jackson how to play ball."

"Ready," LaMont said, "one, two, three . . ."

"Let's go!" shouted the players, raising their hands in the air and breaking the huddle.

As the Patriots ran onto the warped floor in front of only five or six hundred rooters, most of them from Jefferson, Brian felt Coach Ford tap him on the shoulder.

"I hear you handled the ball like Bob Cousy last night," the young coach said, smiling.

"Not quite," Brian said, blushing.

"If you get the chance, try using some of those moves tonight."

"In a real game?" Brian asked.

"Sure, we need to break the press or everybody'll shut us down."

Brian nodded and joined the Patriots' lay-up shooting line. But when he thought about behind-the-back passes and between-the-legs dribbles, his stomach churned nervously.

Twenty minutes later, both starting fives walked to the midcourt jump-ball circle. Alvin Woolridge started as playmaker in place of Terry.

"*Jump, Brian, jump! Jump, Brian, jump!*" shouted Jefferson's cheerleaders. Their voices echoed in the near-empty gym.

Jarvis Poindexter walked over to Brian. "Good luck, man," he said, extending his hand.

Brian shook hands and saw that the six-eight

Jackson center was wearing protective eye goggles like Clarence's.

"Man, he's Reed's big brother," Reggie said, smiling.

Brian looked at Clarence and saw that the muscular senior forward was as mean and determined as ever.

The official tossed up the ball and Poindexter easily won the jump, tapping it to Hoyt Braxton. The six-two playmaker started dribbling toward the Runnin' Rebels' basket.

"I got him," Reggie yelled, crouching into his defensive position.

"Pick up your men," LaMont shouted to the other Patriots.

Brian stayed with Poindexter, who seemed a little confused. The tall Jackson center stood at the top of the key and waved his arms for a pass.

Brian recalled Coach Ford's instructions. He sagged into the foul lane and left Poindexter alone. Almost immediately, Braxton zipped a chest pass to Poindexter, who turned and heaved a twenty-footer at the hoop. The wild shot hit the backboard and fell into Brian's hands.

"Fast break!" Coach Ford shouted from the bench.

"Davis!" Reggie yelled from half court, his hands raised for a pass.

Brian turned toward midcourt and fired a bullet pass to Reggie, who started a fast break. LaMont ran down one side of the court and Alvin raced down the other. Brian knew Reed was back on defense, so he sprinted down the middle of the floor as the trailer on the break, his hands raised.

Reggie stopped at the free-throw line. But the Runnin' Rebels were back on defense. The fast break seemed dead in its tracks, so Brian ran down the left side of the foul lane.

"Dupree!" Brian shouted, his left hand raised.

Reggie looked to the right to get Hoyt Braxton off balance, then scooped a pass to Brian cutting on the left.

Brian grabbed Reggie's perfect pass, took two steps to the basket, and slammed the ball down through the hoop. The Patriots took the early lead 2–0, and their cheerleaders jumped for joy.

"Way to run the break, homeboy," LaMont told Brian.

Braxton began dribbling downcourt for the Rebels, but the ball struck a warped spot on the floor and bounced away. Reggie scooped it up and dribbled back toward Jefferson's hoop.

Brian stopped at midcourt and raced back toward Reggie and the hoop. Poindexter ran alongside him.

"Here!" Brian shouted to Reggie.

Reggie passed the ball to Brian and cut under the basket. Brian caught the ball and faced Poindexter, who was in a defensive stance.

"Put it to him, Davis!" Terry shouted from the bench.

Brian knew he didn't have much time before the other players arrived back downcourt. Almost without thinking, he dribbled twice to his right and got Poindexter leaning that way. Then, just as he'd done the night before with the Mites, he passed the ball around his back to his other hand and dribbled to the basket for a backboard-shaking slam dunk.

The Jefferson rooters stood and cheered. His teammates bashed forearms with him.

"What a move!" Alvin said, laughing.

"Man, you left Poindexter in the dust," Reggie said.

Brian ran downcourt to play defense and saw the stunned looks on the faces of the Jackson players.

For the rest of the opening quarter, the Patriots controlled the game. Jackson didn't press them, and the Jefferson players were able to pass the ball into Brian for jump shots and driving lay-ups past Jarvis Poindexter.

Only Reed, who was overeager and fouled three times, played poorly. Reggie hit two three-pointers while LaMont grabbed five rebounds. At the end of the first quarter, the Patriots led 31–14. Brian had scored fifteen of the Patriots' points.

"Way to handle the ball, guys," Coach Ford said.

"Yeah, nice moves, Davis," Coach Williams added. "But watch out now for Jackson's full-court press."

The Patriots shouted and clapped their hands. The team's spirit was returning after two losses.

George Ross replaced Reed at forward and Jeff Burgess took Brian's spot at center to open the second quarter. Ross prepared to inbound the ball at midcourt and saw the Rebels were lining up in a full-court, man-to-man press.

"Run it," LaMont said, as the Patriots cut into position.

"Jeff's open," Brian said on the bench, pointing at Burgess, who wasn't being pressed well by Poindexter.

Reggie received a pass from Ross and turned toward Burgess downcourt at the top of the key. He fired a chest pass that Jeff caught like a football receiver. Poindexter, burned once by Brian's tricky dribble to the hoop, was playing a few steps back. Burgess seemed unsure what to do and finally dribbled off his foot.

Braxton picked up the loose ball and started a fast break for Jackson.

"Shoot the ball, Burgess," Brian shouted as he ran past the bench.

Downcourt, Braxton swished a three-point jumper, making the score Jefferson 31 and Jackson 17.

The second quarter continued with the Patriots trying to beat the Rebels' full-court press. Reggie, Alvin, and LaMont were successful dribbling downcourt, but Jeff and George fumbled away several passes and dribbled off their feet.

"Davis, get back in there," Coach Ford said. "Handle the ball against the press. Make something happen."

Brian replaced Jeff and immediately the Patriots were pressed all over the court. Brain ran across midcourt and raised his hands. Ross faked a pass to Reggie, then tossed a baseball pass to Brian, who was being closely guarded by Poindexter.

"Davis!" shouted Alvin, streaking downcourt, his hands raised for a pass.

Brian hurled a bullet pass to Alvin, then joined him in a two-on-one fast break against Poindexter.

As they had practiced many times, Brian and Alvin passed the ball and back forth between them while running toward their basket. Poindexter kept backpedaling, staying between the two Patriots as he neared the hoop. He was waiting for his chance to play defense on one of the two attackers.

Brian, running downcourt on the right side, received a pass from Alvin at the top of the key. Poindexter decided to guard Brian closely and leaped out at him in hopes of knocking the ball away. Alvin was unguarded on the left.

Brian dribbled once, then fired a behind-the-back pass to Alvin, who laid in the ball.

The Patriots' subs leaped to their feet and cheered.

"Way to pass, homeboy!" LaMont said, bashing forearms with Brian as they ran downcourt to play defense.

"Man, you oughtta work out with the Mighty Mites more often," Reggie said, laughing.

Later in the second quarter, Brian swished two three-point jumpers over Poindexter, who was playing back expecting a fancy drive to the basket. The next time Brian had the ball in the right corner, Poindexter played up on him to stop the long shot. Brian used some shake-and-bake head and pump fakes and got the six-eight Rebels' center off balance, then drove to the hoop.

Hoyt Braxton and Kenny Gree switched away from their men and double-teamed Brian as he drove along the baseline. When the two defenders attacked him, Brian whipped a behind-the-neck pass to the wide open LaMont, who laid the ball in.

"Nice pass, Davis," LaMont said. "You're dishing out assists like a playmaker."

With Brian and his teammates handling the ball better than they had all season, the Patriots led at halftime 63 to 31, setting a new Jefferson High record for points scored in one half. Brian had twenty-eight of the points as well as ten rebounds. Reggie and George Ross each had scored eleven points, and LaMont had seven rebounds. It was a rout.

Toward the end of the third quarter, with Jefferson leading 83–43, Brian caught a pass from Alvin near midcourt. He started dribbling against the Rebels' playmaker, Hoyt Braxton, who had switched over to guard him.

Hoping for a steal, Braxton lunged toward the ball on Brian's right side. But Brian passed the ball between his own legs to his left side, then tossed it to LaMont cutting down the foul lane for a slam dunk. Braxton fell off balance and Brian left him looking puzzled and embarrassed at midcourt.

The Patriots' subs leaped to their feet.

The Jefferson rooters shouted and applauded.

"Way to move, Davis," Terry yelled from the bench.

Brian finished the third quarter trying more of his newly-learned ball-handling moves. Most of the tricky maneuvers worked, and he lost the ball out-of-bounds only once. The team had improved its ball-handling enough to stomp all over the Runnin' Rebels.

Brian scored thirty-nine points and grabbed fourteen rebounds in only three quarters. Then, he and the other starters rested on the bench for the entire last quarter while Ross, Burgess, and the subs got some badly needed experience. The final score was the Patriots 107 and Jackson 60.

"Man, a school record for points in a game," Reggie said in the happy locker room after the game.

"Yeah, and we got us a new playmaker in Davis," Tony said, bashing forearms with Brian.

"Homeboy was something else," LaMont added.

Brian just smiled and enjoyed the cheers and laughter of a winning locker room again.

TEN

"I'll join the Mighty Mites if that's what it takes," Reggie said. "Man, you see what they taught Davis?"

"Yeah, but Davis thinks like a ten-year-old," Tony added with a smile. "That's his secret."

It was a chilly Saturday afternoon, and Brian and his two best friends were walking to the middle school where the Mighty Mites practiced The glow of the Patriots' big win against Jackson the night before continued to warm them as they neared the school.

"How can a bunch of ten-year-olds do it?" Reggie asked, pulling his knit cap farther down on his head.

"Like the dude says in that TV commercial, Dupree," Tony said, "practice, practice, practice."

"Zarella's right," Brian said, walking to the

middle school's front door. "Look what I did after only one day's practice. Heck, even you oughtta be able to learn how, Dupree."

"Man, those dribbling tricks ain't gonna work against good teams," Reggie said.

"Yeah, Jackson's players were a bunch of scrubs," Tony added. "Dudes didn't know how to play defense."

Brian opened the door and the three teammates walked toward the shouts and dribbling sounds in the gym.

"I know," Brian said, "but doing these ball-handling moves makes your regular dribbling better, too."

"That's cool," Reggie said. "Let me see these Mighty Mite dudes."

Brian and his friends walked into the gym. Bobby Gutheridge saw them and waved. Ricky and Teddy, the kids who'd played against Brian in the park, stopped their dribbling drills and greeted the three Patriots.

"Glad you three could make it," the dark-haired Gutheridge said, smiling, and pointing at two guys in their twenties who were shooting baskets. "I brought along a couple of friends for a scrimmage later on. You know, half court, three against three."

Brian nodded, and then he and his friends warmed up by dribbling with the Mites.

"We're putting on a dribbling exhibition tonight at Butler fieldhouse," Ricky told Brian in his high-pitched little kid's voice. "You guys comin' to watch?"

"Some of the fathers can't make it tonight," Gutheridge said, cutting in. "You can have their tickets if you want. Butler plays Ball State, so the game'll be good."

"Man, I never turn down free tickets," Reggie said.

Gutheridge and the others laughed.

For the next twenty minutes, Brian used the Mites' practice to sharpen his new ball-handling skills. At the same time, Reggie and Tony learned all about the little kids' dribbling drills.

"Spread your legs wider," little Ricky said to Tony as they practiced between-the-legs dribbling.

"Wrap your passing arm around your back when you throw the ball," Teddy told Reggie when they worked on behind-the-back passing.

The Mites practiced alongside the three boys from Jefferson as well.

"These dudes know what they're talking about, Davis," Reggie said, practicing a few between-the-legs dribbles.

"I can't wait to try these moves in a game," Tony added. He passed his ball behind his back and followed with a between-the-legs dribble to his other hand.

"You gotta wait a week, Zarella," Brian said.

"Yeah, exams come first," Reggie said sadly.

Ricky walked over to them.

"Wanna try our routine?" he asked.

"You mean spinning the ball and that stuff?" Brian asked, hoping he was wrong.

"Go ahead, Davis," Reggie said, "show 'em how it's done."

"This is the routine the kids use for their dribbling exhibitions," Gutheridge explained as the Mites lined up.

Brian took his place at the end of the line and followed the Mighty Mites onto the court.

"Spin the ball on your finger, Davis," Ricky told him as they formed a circle at midcourt.

Brian tried to keep his ball spinning on his right index finger, but it rolled off several times.

Reggie and Tony laughed along the sidelines.

"No sweat, just follow us," Ricky told Brian as the Mites began dribbling up and down the court, passing their basketballs around their backs and between their legs. To his surprise, Brian did it, too.

"Hey, look at Davis," Reggie said, pointing.

"He's a regular Mighty Mite," Tony added.

Brian's two teammates continued to laugh until Gutheridge waved them onto the floor and into the drills.

"Come on, guys, let's see what you got," he said.

Reggie and Tony looked nervous as they started following the Mites' dribbling routine. Reggie bounced his ball off his foot twice and Tony passed wildly around his back.

"Ain't so easy, eh, boys?" Brian said, laughing now.

Fifteen minutes later, the Mites finished their practice session and left the gym to rest up for their exhibition that night. Brian and his two teammates stayed to play a three-on-three half court scrimmage against Gutheridge and his friends.

"First team to score twenty baskets wins," Gutheridge said, passing the ball to Brian. "When you score, you keep the ball until you miss or the defense stops you."

Brian passed the ball to Reggie, who was being guarded by a six-two white guy who looked pretty quick. Tony's man was a five-nine balding black guy who seemed lost on the court. Gutheridge was guarding Brian.

The Patriots worked a few pick and roll plays until finally Brian was free for a jumper, which he swished.

"Way to shoot, bro," Reggie said.

"Davis can make 'em," Gutheridge told his two buddies, "so get out on him."

The Patriots ran the same plays, but this time, when Brian was open for a fifteen-foot jump shot, the balding guy jumped out at him and guarded him closely. Brian up-faked with the ball to get the defender off his feet, then drove to the basket along the baseline. Gutheridge switched over to guard Brian and cut off his path to the hoop.

Without stopping, Brian whipped a behind-the-back pass to Reggie in the foul lane, who swished a short jumper.

"Nice pass," Gutheridge said to Brian, patting him on the back. "That's the way to use your ball-handling skills."

The scrimmage continued for twenty minutes until finally Brian and his teammates won 20–12. Gutheridge had scored most of his team's hoops, while all of the Patriots had used their new ball-handling moves to score easy baskets.

"Man, I feel like a new player with these moves," Reggie said, toweling off.

"Don't get carried away," Gutheridge told him. "Too many fancy moves can get you in trouble."

"Unless you're passing to me, Dupree," Brian said with a grin. "Then you can use all the behind-the-back stuff you want."

"This fieldhouse is something else," Reggie said, looking around Butler's Hinkle fieldhouse that evening.

"Yeah, it's old and drafty," Tony said.

"Man, it's a great place to play ball," Reggie said.

"If you like playing in an airplane hangar," Tony said.

"Maybe we'll get a chance to shoot around after Butler's game," Brian said as they found their seats on one end of the court.

The fieldhouse soon was half-filled with Butler Bulldog fans. The University's band played and the teams trotted onto the brightly-lit floor for their warm-ups.

Later, as Tony munched nachos and a hotdog, Brian and his teammates watched Butler fall behind early to a scrappy Ball State team and trail at half time, 52–36.

"Ball State's full-court press hurt Butler," Brian mentioned. "They could've used the Mites' dribbling moves."

"Speaking of the Mighty Mites," Tony said, swallowing the last of his second hotdog, "here they come."

Brian looked along with the thousands of other fans as Ricky led the Mites onto the court for their ball-handling exhibition. The PA announcer gave the boys a loud introduction.

"They're doing everything they showed us today," Reggie said. "They're great!"

When they finished their half-time routine, the crowd gave them a standing ovation.

"That's more applause than we get," Tony said, clapping with everybody else.

"The dudes deserve it," Reggie said.

The three Patriots settled down and started to watch the second half when they heard somebody yelling insults at them.

"Davis and Jefferson stink!"

"You guys are lucky wimps!"

Reggie stood. "Say what?" he said.

They looked around and saw four smiling high-school kids with the crowd returning from the concession stands.

"Who are those dudes?" Reggie asked.

"It's that jerk Barry Ellis and his friends from Morris Central," Tony said.

"Hey, don't we play 'em at home next Friday?" Brian asked as he watched the four laughing kids disappear around a corner.

"Yeah, but they're a bunch of geeks," Tony said, sitting again.

"They got a six-ten dude named Dun Mitchell," Reggie said, "but the kid's only a sophomore and falls over his own feet."

"You oughtta eat him alive, Davis," Tony added.

"What about Ellis?" Brian asked.

"The jerk talks a good fight, but even I can outplay him," Tony said, turning his attention to the game.

"That shows you how bad the dude really is," Reggie said, playfully punching Tony on the arm.

Ball State pressed Butler all over the court in the second half and forced most of the ball-handling errors. Butler played poorly on defense, too, and lost 105–74.

After the crowd left the fieldhouse, Bobby Gutheridge showed up with three of the Mighty Mites' red-white-and-blue basketballs. Brian and his friends shot for half an hour, until the maintenance men shut off the lights and drove them off the court.

"Butler should've learned some ball-handling tricks from the Mites," Reggie told Gutheridge when they gave him back the balls. "Ball State's press ate 'em alive."

"I know," Gutheridge said with a smile, "but the college players think they know it all. They figure a bunch of ten-year-old kids can't teach 'em anything new."

"They taught me something," Tony said.

"Me, too," Reggie added with a smile, "Now, I know I'm another Magic Johnson."

He laughed, and his teammates shoved him playfully.

Later, at the Hamburger Heaven, Brian and his friends stuffed themselves with cheeseburgers and fries.

"Zarella, where do you put all that food?" Reggie said, shaking his head.

"My legs are hollow," said Tony, finishing off an order of fries swimming in ketchup.

"So's your head," Reggie said, tossing a fry at Tony.

Suddenly, a shower of french fries rained down on Brian and his two teammates.

"Hey!" Tony said.

"What the . . . ?" Brian said, looking up.

They saw the four Morris Central kids, led by Barry Ellis, laughing and tossing french fries at them from the other side of the crowded fast-food restaurant.

"Man, I'm gonna . . ." Reggie said, standing.

"No," Brian said, grabbing Dupree's shirt.

It was too late. Reggie grabbed a handful of fries and tossed them across the dining room. Several adult patrons screamed and covered their faces.

"Food fight!" shouted Barry Ellis, the five-ten Morris Central player. He grabbed a ketchup container.

"Get 'em, guys!" shouted another Central kid.

"Don't do it, Reg," Brian said, holding Dupree's arms away from his food. "It'll only mean trouble."

The Morris Central kids squirted ketchup and mustard at Brian and his friends, accidentally splattering some adults in the process. People screamed. The manager ran into the dining room, and Ellis and his laughing buddies escaped quickly through the restaurant's side door.

"Sir, they started it," Tony explained to the manager a few minutes later. But it didn't do them any good.

Brian, Tony, and Reggie agreed to clean up the dining room if the manager promised not to call the police.

"Man, wait until we get Ellis and those guys on the court," Reggie said, sponging away some ketchup from their booth.

"This is disgusting," Tony said, wiping some ketchup from his shirt.

"Next Friday," Brian said, mopping up mustard from the floor. "That's the night we get our revenge."

"Keep down the noise and clean up that mess," the manager shouted at them.

Brian and his friends nodded and continued to work.

ELEVEN

"My brain is strung out," Reggie said, joining the Patriot players in the cafeteria on Monday. "And I didn't even take my algebra final yet."

"Man, I got my biology exam next period," Alvin said, shaking his head as he pored over some notes.

"That's nothin'," Clarence said. "I just finished the meanest English final ever."

"Hi, guys," Brad said, adjusting his glasses and sitting down with a tray full of food. "I aced my calculus final."

The other Patriots booed and shoved Cunningham around playfully.

"Hey, brain, you wanna take my history exam for me?" Terry asked from across the table. He had his U.S. history book and pages of notes spread out on the table.

"Hanson, you gonna pass that final?" Reggie asked.

"Sure, he is," Brian said, biting into an apple. "The dude had a great tutor."

"Naw, it was your aunt's chocolate chip cookies that did it, Davis," Tony said, smiling.

It was the first day of final exam week, and Brian and his teammates were struggling through the day. They were especially interested in how Reggie and Terry did, and whether the two of them would be eligible for hoops by the end of the week.

"Wish we had a game tomorrow," Terry said. "I'm sick of studying. I need to get back on the court."

"Bro, you're lucky Coach let you outta practice today and tomorrow," LaMont said. "Coach Williams is gonna run everybody's butts off with his special drills."

"Thanks for reminding us, Jackson," Brian said, thinking about the zigzag drill and the others.

"Yeah, I wanna be ready for those dorks Barry Ellis and Morris Central on Friday night," Reggie said.

"And that plane trip to East Bend Central next Tuesday," Tony added.

"I hate flyin'," Reed said.

"Let's beat Ellis and Morris Central first," La-Mont said as the bell rang.

"We'll get 'em on Friday," Terry said.

"Man, you just think about your history final, or there won't be no Friday for you," Reggie said to Hanson.

The Patriots walked to their classes, and Brian was glad his grades were good. The pressure from the upcoming state tournament was going to be all he could handle.

At practice on Monday and Tuesday, the biggest news was that both Reggie and Terry passed their exams. All that week, Brian and his teammates worked hard on Coach Williams's ball-handling drills.

"We don't want anybody's press to bother us the rest of the season."

Friday's game finally arrived, and the Patriots were psyched.

The Jefferson High gym was packed, the cheerleaders were shouting, and in the locker room there was some serious planning going on.

"I'm gonna kick Ellis on his butt," Reggie said.

"We owe him one," Tony added, straightening the wrinkles in his white home uniform.

"These Morris Central dudes never did have no class," Reed said, cleaning his goggles.

"Best way to show 'em up is to beat 'em bad," Coach Williams said as he and Coach Ford joined the team.

"All right, coach!" Terry shouted, bashing forearms with Reggie and Tony.

"But you gotta be prepared," Coach Ford added, looking at the Morris Central scouting report on his clipboard. He glanced at the Patriots.

"Davis, their center is a six-ten black sophomore named Dun Mitchell," Coach Ford said. "The kid's gonna be good someday, but right now he's uncoordinated and can't shoot."

"Betcha the dude knows how to throw french fries," Reggie said, bashing forearms with Tony.

The team laughed, then looked at Coach Ford again.

"Their best player is Lamar Reynolds, a six-five forward," the coach continued.

"I know the dude," LaMont said, pulling on his blue warm-up jacket. "He's a brother from my side of town. He likes long three-point shots, but he's slow."

"He's all yours, LaMont," Coach Ford said.

"Who gets that Ellis dude?" Reggie asked.

Coach Ford smiled. "We saved him for you, Dupree."

"Shut him down, Reg," Brian said.

"The rest of their players are average," Coach Ford concluded, "so play your usual tough man-to-man and you'll stop 'em."

The B team game ended in the gym.

"Guys, we have only two more games after tonight before the tournament," Coach Ford said finally.

Brian saw the serious expressions on the faces of his teammates. Tournament time in Indiana was big stuff.

"We've worked hard all season," the coach continued. "I think we're gonna go far. We gotta win tonight."

"Man, we're gonna be state champs," Clarence said, pulling his goggles over his eyes and smiling at everybody.

"All right!" shouted several of the players.

Brian and the Patriots' usual starting five were super-psyched by the time they walked to the midcourt circle for the opening jump ball. Morris Central's starting lineup, dressed in maroon away uniforms, joined them.

"Eaten any junk food lately?" Barry Ellis asked as he walked past Brian.

Hal Brodsky, Central's six-three white forward, laughed. Brian recognized him as one of the four kids at the restaurant.

"Ignore 'em, bro," LaMont told Brian. "We'll show 'em on the court."

"They don't bother me," Brian said, preparing to jump.

"They bother *me*," Reggie said, glaring at Ellis.

Brian shook hands with Mitchell, and then an official tossed up the ball between them. Despite being shorter, Brian out-jumped Mitchell easily and tapped the ball to Terry. He dribbled toward their basket.

"Zone!" shouted Terry, recognizing the type of defense Morris Central was playing. "It's a two-three."

Brian ran to the baseline and began the Patriots' offense against a zone.

"Look for good shots," Coach Ford shouted at them.

Terry zipped an overhead pass to Reggie on the right, and he snapped a chest pass to LaMont on the right baseline. Brian saw the Morris Central defenders were reacting slowly and sneaked under the basket.

"Hey!" he shouted, raising his hands.

LaMont snapped an overhead pass to Brian, who laid in the ball. Jefferson led, 2–0.

"Pick 'em up!" LaMont yelled at his teammates, and the Patriots pressed all over the court.

Brodsky tried to inbound the ball for Central, but all his teammates were being closely guarded. Finally, he tossed a wild lob pass toward Mitchell in front of the Patriots' basket. Brian leaped and intercepted the pass.

Barry Ellis and Brodsky quickly double-teamed him.

"Davis!" Reggie shouted, cutting down the lane.

Brian faked up with the ball and the two Central defenders leaped like puppets on a string. Then he zipped a behind-the-back pass to Reggie, who slammed-dunked the ball with gusto.

The Jefferson cheerleaders leaped and yelled.

"All right!" LaMont shouted, waving at Brian and the others to continue their full-court man-to-man press.

Brodsky grabbed the ball out of bounds again, but, instead of looking for a teammate close to him, he launched a long baseball pass downcourt that Terry intercepted at the midcourt line.

The redheaded senior dribbled toward the Patriots' hoop. He kept his head up and bounced the ball low.

"Hanson!" Brian shouted, cutting along the base line.

But Terry was suddenly closely guarded by Barry Ellis and passed the ball to Reggie, who turned and looked at Ellis.

"Lose him, Dupree," Tony shouted from the bench.

"No way," Ellis said, smiling as he crouched and began guarding Reggie.

Dupree dribbled quickly to the right of the Patriots' basket, but Ellis raced ahead and cut him off. Reggie smiled and bounce-passed the ball between his legs to his other hand, then dribbled to the left leaving Ellis behind.

The Jefferson rooters cheered the fancy play.

Reggie dribbled down the lane and got double-teamed by Brodsky and Mitchell.

Both Brian and LaMont were free for a pass.

The double-team tried to smother Reggie in the lane, but he hooked a behind-the-back pass to Brian on the left of the hoop. When the defenders turned and leaped at Brian, he flipped a behind-the-neck pass to LaMont. The Patriots' captain slam-dunked the ball.

After only a minute of play, Jefferson led 6–0.

"Nice pass, bro," LaMont said to Brian.

The rest of the first quarter belonged to the Patriots. Except for two three-pointers by Central's Lamar Reynolds, Brian and his teammates passed and shot better than they had all season.

In addition to their tricky moves, the Patriots showed they could dribble with their heads up and control the ball while being closely guarded. The score after one quarter was Jefferson 30 and Morris Central 12.

"You oughtta stick to throwing french fries," Reggie told Ellis as the teams walked to their benches.

Brian saw the anger in Ellis's eyes.

"You tell him, Dupree," Terry said.

"Yeah, the dude didn't score a point," Tony added.

The second quarter began with Jeff Burgess in for Brian, George Ross for Clarence, and Alvin for Terry. And, except for Ross's hot shooting, the subs let Central back in the game. Reynolds drove past Jeff for three baskets and a couple of free throws, and Ellis scored twice on long jumpers. Reed returned, replacing LaMont, but Central continued to catch up as Clarence fouled Mitchell three times.

Taking advantage of Reggie's new ball-handling skill, Ross received half a dozen sharp passes and scored on long jump shots and driving lay-ups. He even swished two three-point bombs, grabbed four rebounds, and blocked a shot by Ellis.

"Eat that, Ellis," Brian shouted from the bench.

"Yeah, and hold the mustard," Tony added, laughing.

Brian returned to the game midway in the quarter and continued to out-play the slow moving Mitchell. He swished a hook shot, made a three-pointer from the corner, and passed to George Ross for an easy lay-up over Ellis. At half time, the score was Jefferson 61 and Morris Central 35.

Ellis, Brodsky, and the other Central players raced to their locker room, obviously embarrassed.

The Patriots dominated Central in the second half. Brian used his shake-and-bake moves on offense to score against Mitchell, and he passed like a playmaker when Central tried another full-court press. Coach Ford let everybody play, and even the subs played well.

The final score was Jefferson 100 and Morris Central 72. The Patriots had scored one hundred or more points for the second game in a row, and their win-loss record improved to 14 and 4, with only two games remaining to play.

"Ellis didn't even shake our hands after the game," Tony said in the locker room.

"Man, the dude ran off the court like a scared rabbit," Reggie said, laughing.

Brian had played less than three quarters, but he scored 37 points and pulled down 14 rebounds. George Ross played his best game of the year off the bench, scoring twenty-four points.

"We're heading back to the top twenty," Terry shouted.

The Patriots cheered, until LaMont held up his hand.

"We gotta beat East Bend Central first," said the captain, mentioning next Tuesday's game. "Then we'll deserve being in the top twenty."

TWELVE

"Man, this plane is small," Reggie said as the Patriots stood on the runway of the Indianapolis airport. They were looking at the team's chartered DC-3 propeller plane.

"I hope it flies," Tony said.

"Hey, did you guys see the movie *La Bamba*," Terry asked, looking up at the falling snow flurries.

"You mean when Ritchie Valens and those guys took off in a snowstorm?" Brian asked.

"Yeah, and then the plane crashed in a cornfield," Terry continued.

The Patriots booed and shoved Hanson playfully.

"Man, don't talk like that," Clarence said. "I hate flyin'."

It was Tuesday afternoon and the Patriots were

124

preparing to fly to East Bend in northern Indiana. The East Bend Central Blue Devils were ranked number eleven in the state, and Brian and his teammates were looking forward to playing a highly ranked team again.

Following Friday's easy win, the Jefferson rooters were starting to get 'tourney fever' as they looked forward to the state tournament. A win over Central would boost school spirit for weeks.

But they weren't too keen on flying to and from the game on the same day—and in snow flurries.

"Hey, Coach Ford," Tony said, "what's wrong with taking a bus? This plane doesn't look too safe."

"Zarella, the DC-3 is one of the world's safest planes," the coach said, leading the Patriots on board.

The one-hour flight was smooth, and even Clarence enjoyed himself once he opened his eyes and looked out the window. As they neared the East Bend airport, Brian concentrated on Central's players. Coach Ford reviewed the Blue Devils' scouting report over the drone of the DC-3's engines.

"Butch Harris, a tough six-seven black forward, is Central's best player," Coach Ford said, looking at his notes.

"'Basketball Magazine' rated him one of the top ten high school players in the country," Brian said, remembering the article in his basketball magazine back home.

"Dude must have all the moves," Reggie said.

"He shoots well from outside and knows all the shake-and-bake stuff," Coach Williams said.

"It's hard to stop a guy like Harris," Coach Ford added. "LaMont'll just have to play as tough as he can."

"What about their center?" Brian shouted over the engine noise.

"Name's Ralph Radowski," Coach Ford said, "and he's a six-eight senior who looks like a football tackle."

"Weigh two hundred-and-eighty pounds," Coach Willaims said, smiling at Brian.

"Man, dude'll squash Davis," Reggie said, laughing.

"Just do your best keeping him away from the boards," Coach Ford told Brian. "He's slow and weak on defense. Doesn't move his feet and can't jump much, either."

"And the guards?" Terry asked.

"They're all quick," Coach Ford said, "and that's why they press in the backcourt."

"Their top guard is a five-ten white kid named Larry Sadecki," Coach Williams added. "On defense, don't let him shoot unguarded three-pointers. He's one of the best bombers in the state."

"We can play with these guys," Coach Ford concluded, putting away his clipboard. "But we gotta handle the ball well against their press and play smart on defense."

Brian felt his stomach churning with anticipation already, and he liked the feeling. It meant he was ready.

The plane landed without a problem, and the Patriots rode a chartered school bus to the East Bend Central gym in the middle of the smoky, soot-covered industrial city.

"Man, smell that air," Reggie said, holding his nose.

"That's sulfur, Dupree," Coach Williams said. "Lots of steel mills up here."

"I ain't never gonna complain about the air in Indianapolis again," Clarence said, sniffing and making a face.

They arrived at the big gym and watched East Bend Central's girls team demolish a shorter, less talented team in the preliminary game. When it was time for both boys teams to head for the locker rooms to change into their uniforms, Brian and his teammates were stunned when big Ralph Radowski, the 280-pound East Bend center, walked past them along with the other Blue Devils.

"Man, dude looks like a pro wrestler," Reggie said.

"Good luck with him, Davis," Terry said, laughing.

Brian smiled. "If he gets past me, Hanson, I'm looking for you to switch over and pick him up."

The Patriots laughed, and Terry shook his head.

Brian and his teammates, dressed in their blue away uniforms, ran onto the court in front of five thousand screaming Blue Devil rooters. The Jefferson cheerleaders didn't make the long trip, so Brian and the Patriots felt alone amid the cheering East Bend fans.

After the introductions, Brian and the usual starting five lined up for the opening jump ball. East Bend's starters joined them, and Brian shook hands with Ralph Radowski, staring at how wide and muscular the Blue Devil center was.

"You can out-jump him, homeboy," LaMont said in Brian's ear. "Look for me or Reggie."

Brian nodded, then leaped as high as he could when the official tossed up the ball between him and Radowski. East Bend's big center barely got off the floor, and Brian easily tapped the ball to LaMont on the right.

"Jackson!" Reggie shouted as he raced away from the jump-ball circle, his hands raised for a pass.

LaMont turned and tossed a perfect lead pass toward the Patriots' basket, but five-ten Larry Sadecki sprinted back on defense for the Blue Devils and intercepted it.

"These guys aren't Morris Central or some other geeks," Terry said as he ran back on defense with Brian.

"We can take 'em," LaMont said.

Brian ran over to Radowski and tried to reach around the massive center to knock away a pass from Sadecki. The officials blew their whistles and pointed at Brian.

"Reaching-in foul on number fifty in the blue," said one of the refs, calling Brian for a foul.

Coach Ford protested from the bench, but the call stood.

East Bend inbounded the ball and tried again to pass the ball into Radowski. Brian played back and the big center caught the ball, turned, and missed an easy ten-foot jumper. Brian turned and thought the rebound was going to be his, but suddenly six-seven forward Butch Harris appeared out of nowhere and tapped the ball into the basket.

East Bend led 2–0, and the gym rocked with the loud cheers of their fans.

"My fault," LaMont said. "I should've blocked Harris away from the boards."

"Dude's too quick," Clarence said, grabbing the ball and preparing to pass it inbounds.

Brian and his teammates ran downcourt to play offense, but, as they did, they looked back to see if East Bend was using some sort of press. Brian noticed Sadecki and Ryerson, East Bend's other guard, were getting ready to smother Reggie and Terry in the backcourt. Reed yelled for help and slapped the ball.

"Here!" Reggie yelled, his hand raised.

Reed passed the ball to Reggie, who turned and tried a behind-the-back dribble against Sadecki. The Blue Devil playmaker lashed out with his right hand and stole the ball in the middle of Dupree's fancy move. He passed it to Ryerson, who laid it in for a score.

"Save those moves for later," Brian shouted to Reggie, who nodded, "Pass the ball."

Reed inbounded the ball again, and this time Brian and the Patriots worked their press play correctly. They got the ball across midcourt and worked a play against East Bend's man-to-man half-court defense.

Brian cut to the free-throw line, leaving the slow Radowski behind him, and caught a pass from Terry. Brian then turned and lofted a soft fifteen-foot jumper toward the basket that swished through the cotton cords. But Radowski recovered late and tried to block the ball. He smashed into Brian after the shot and sent him sprawling backwards on the floor.

It felt like Brian had been hit by a train.

"You okay, Davis?" Reggie asked, helping him to his feet.

Brian cleared his head and nodded. "The guy thinks he's playing football," he said, looking at Radowski, who was smiling.

Brian swished his free-throw and the score was East Bend 4 and Jefferson 3.

The first quarter continued with Butch Harris scoring easily over and around LaMont and everybody else who tried to stop his super-quick moves to the hoop. For Jefferson, Brian noticed Radowski wasn't playing him closely away from the basket, so he swished two three-point jumpers in a row. East Bend's press didn't bother the Patriots as long as Reggie kept his fancy ball-handling moves under control. And the Patriots knew how to handle the ball now.

The score after one quarter was East Bend 23 and Jefferson 18. Harris had twelve points, Brian scored ten.

"I can get past Harris," LaMont said as he wiped his face with a towel. "The dude can't stop my drives."

"Okay," Coach Ford shouted above the noise of

the East Bend rooters, "look for Brian underneath or LaMont for some drives. You're doing a great job handling the ball."

The second quarter opened with Sadecki tossing a pass to Butch Harris, who faked LaMont out of his jock on his way to the hoop. Brian waited until the last moment, leaped away from Radowski, and blocked Harris' lay-up attempt. Reggie picked up the loose ball and started a Patriot fast break.

"In your face," Reed shouted at Harris, who was stunned by the blocked shot.

Without waiting for congratulations, Brian turned and sprinted down the right sideline as one of the wings of the fast break. Reggie stopped at the free-throw line, faked a pass to Terry on the left, and scooped an underhand pass to Brian cutting to the hoop on the right. Brian slammed the ball down through the basket.

"Way to go, homeboy!" Clarence shouted a they ran back downcourt. He bashed forearms with Brian.

After his slam dunk, Brian noticed a little more respect for the Patriots in the eyes of the East Bend Blue Devils. The rest of the half saw Brian and his teammates do as well as they could against Butch Harris, while stopping the other Devils from shooting or passing effectively. On offense, Brian swished two more three-pointer jump shots over Radowski's hands and LaMont drove around Harris for three easy baskets and some free throws.

At the end of the first half, Jefferson had

grabbed the lead, 42–38. Brian had scored twenty points while high school All-American Butch Harris totaled nineteen.

After Coach Ford reviewed their strategy, the Patriots took the floor for the second half. Brian noticed the angry looks on the faces of Radowski and the other Devils.

Less than a minute into the half, East Bend's new strategy was obvious. Radowski began shoving and elbowing Brian at every opportunity, keeping him off balance when he received passes from Reggie or Terry.

"He's fouling me," Brian said, after Radowski nearly pushed him off the court.

"Be cool, homeboy," LaMont said. "The refs aren't gonna help us here."

"It's home cookin'," Terry said.

"It's dirty ball," Brian said, starting to lose his temper. Then he cooled down. "Let's beat 'em, anyway," he said finally.

The third quarter turned into a war as the East Bend players whacked, shoved, and elbowed the Patriots whenever they could. Still, Brian and his teammates kept their cool and handled the ball like never before. Halfway through the period, East Bend stopped pressing because the Patriots were beating it so often for easy lay-ups downcourt.

Because of Radowski's rough style of play, Brian became more of a passer on offense than a scorer. On many occasions, he whipped bullet passes to Reggie, LaMont, and Terry for lay-ups or jumpers. And, when he did manage some room to shoot, he swished two long jumpers over Radowski.

The roughhouse style of play worked most of the time for the Blue Devils, and after three quarters, they regained the lead, 62–61. Brian felt like he'd been in a street fight, and his arms ached from being whacked.

"Games are won or lost in the last quarter," LaMont told the Patriots as they walked back onto the floor.

"Yeah, look at Harris, Radowski, and the rest of 'em," Terry said. "They're dragging their butts."

"Let's run 'em into the floor," said Brian, wondering where he was going to get the energy to do it.

As Reed prepared to toss in the ball to open the final quarter, Radowski walked over to Brian with a mean look on his face.

"You guys ain't gonna win," said the 280-pounder in a voice resembling a growl. "I ain't gonna let you."

"Cool it, fat boy," Reggie said, as he walked past Radowski.

Brian watched the East Bend center's face turn red with anger. Harris and Sadecki struggled to keep Radowski from charging after Reggie.

"Hey, Dupree," Brian said quietly, "you're picking on the wrong guy."

"Dude's a wimp," Reggie said, smiling up at Brian.

Brian wondered about Reggie's choice of words until Radowski made mistake after mistake during the opening moments of the last quarter.

At the same time, Brian and the Patriots worked their plays against the Devils' man-to-man defense. Brian scored on a drive past the enraged Radowski, and Clarence rebounded one of Brian's missed jumpers and stuffed it into the hoop.

With a minute to go, the score was East Bend 80 and Jefferson 79. The Patriots had the ball.

"Come on, hotshot," Radowski growled, playing defense to the right of the basket, "show me your stuff."

Brian saw the sweat pouring off the massive center's broad, fleshy face. Then he felt Rodowski's elbow digging into his chest and his other hand grabbing his jersey.

Terry called a play and raised his hand.

Reed turned and set a pick on Radowski, who grunted when he smashed into Clarence. Brian cut through the foul lane and caught a sharp chest pass from Hanson.

Butch Harris, an angry look on his face that told Brian he was going for a blocked shot, leaped toward Brian and left LaMont unguarded on the right. Brian whipped a behind-the-neck pass with his left hand to LaMont, who scored a lay-up, giving the Patriots the lead, 81–80.

Only twenty-four seconds remained in the game.

"Pick up your men!" LaMont shouted. "No fouls!"

Brian and his teammates quickly pressed the Devils.

With ten seconds remaining on the scoreboard

clock, Radowski caught a pass from Sadecki but couldn't control his dribble. Brian picked up the loose ball and started to dribble away the seconds.

The time ticked away: 0:09, 0:08, 0:07.

Harris, Sadecki, and the entire East Bend team began chasing Brian in hopes of stealing the ball and shooting a last-second, game-winning shot. But Brian dribbled like a playmaker.

Sadecki tried for a steal, but Brian used a behind-the-back dribble to get away from him. Harris reached in for a steal, but Brian passed the ball between his own legs to his other hand. Suddenly, he spotted LaMont free under the Patriots' basket and passed behind his back to their captain, who laid the ball in as the buzzer sounded. The final score was Jefferson 83 and East Bend 80.

The Patriots on the bench joined the starters at midcourt to celebrate their victory over the top-rated Blue Devils.

"All right, Davis!" Cisco yelled, bashing forearms. "We're back in the top twenty!"

"Yeah," Reggie added, "and nothing can stop us now!"

The whole team followed Dupree, raised their fists in the air, and shouted. "Patriots rule!"

The pressure is really on center Brian Davis as he leads the Jefferson Patriots to the State Tournament in the next action-packed book:

HOOPS #5: TOURNEY FEVER